7/11

The Christmas Hope

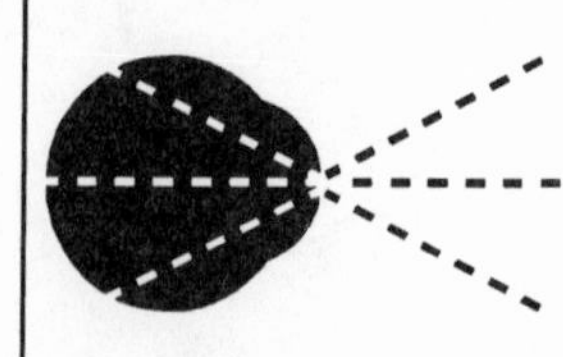

This Large Print Book carries the Seal of Approval of N.A.V.H.

The Christmas Hope

Donna VanLiere

THORNDIKE PRESS
An imprint of Thomson Gale, a part of The Thomson Corporation

Detroit • New York • San Francisco • New Haven, Conn. • Waterville, Maine • London

Thorndike Press® Large Print Americana.

The text of this Large Print edition is unabridged.

Other aspects of the book may vary from the original edition.

Set in 16 pt. Plantin.

LIBRARY OF CONGRESS CATALOGING-IN-PUBLICATION DATA

VanLiere, Donna, 1966–
The Christmas hope / by Donna Vanliere.
p. cm. — (Thorndike Press large print Americana)
ISBN 0-7862-8766-7 (hardcover : alk. paper)
1. Women social workers — Fiction. 2. Married people — Fiction. 3. Girls — Fiction. 4. Christmas stories. 5. Large type books. I. Title. II. Series: Thorndike Press large print Americana series.
PS3622.A66C478 2006
813'.6—dc22 2006016451

ISBN 13: 978-0-7862-8766-6

Published in 2006 by arrangement with St. Martin's Press, LLC.

Printed in the United States of America on permanent paper
10 9 8 7 6 5 4 3 2 1

For Kate,
whose smile proves the existence
of Hope

ACKNOWLEDGMENTS

Much appreciation and thanks to . . .

Troy, for always listening to my ideas and then being the first to cheer me on to completion. (By the way, I still maintain that it doesn't make you a coauthor just because you suggest one word in a manuscript.)

Kate, you have filled this house with your tiny laugh. Thank you for your sweet smile, kisses, and the joy that overtakes your body when you see your mom and dad in the "mor-nie!" What would our home be without you in it?

Gracie, you are the "good big sister." Thank you for all the nights you spend in "Mommy-Daddy bed" reading, laughing, singing, and snuggling, and for always wanting to help me cook and bake cookies! Yes, you are a "good big helper," too.

Jennifer Gates, for your ready ear, wise direction, and sweet stories of Jack. He's blessed to have you as his mother. Hopefully, one day I'll get around to writing all those books we talk about.

Esmond Harmsworth, I appreciate the time you take to read over each manuscript, the feedback and guidance you give, and the great stories of your childhood. There's a book for you!

Jennifer Enderlin, I'm grateful for your belief in me and for being my cheerleader at St. Martin's. Welcome, Nicholas! Thanks, too, to the marketing and sales staff for all your efforts.

Chris and Tonya Carter (welcome Connor and Eli!), Chad and Sherry Carter, Tony and Kathy Dupree, David and Marilyn Knight, and everyone at the Orchard Church for your encouragement, friendship, and faithfulness.

Beth Grossbard, you said you had a vision for *The Christmas Blessing* and you wouldn't stop working until it became reality. Thank you. I can't wait to see the movie! You are a great encourager. Craig Anderson, thank you also for your belief and support. We are honored to work with both you and Beth.

Dr. Ann Kavanaugh-McHugh (with Vanderbilt Children's Hospital Division of Pediatric Cardiology), for sharing your time and knowledge with me again. You are very gracious.

My nephews and niece, Patrick and Tyler Payne, Joshua Richmond, and Alyssa and Desmond VanLiere, who are growing up to be fine young people.

Tonya Carter, Hannah Fennell, and Lauren Wilcox for loving our girls during the time you've each watched them, and Nancy Townsend for being ready at a moment's notice for those quick trips to the doctor's office. Hannah, we miss you. Do well in college!

Big hugs to Emmie Kate Boucher, Brady Carter, Becky and Kaki Catalano, Emily Cullimore, Zara and Zena Dorris, Isabella Hamm, Abby Lee, Abby and Laura Newell, Nathan Ogden, Sarah Ottinger, Zoe and Ava Pryor (we miss you), Caitlin Townsend, and Jenny Wooten for your giggles, smiles, and sweet play dates together.

"Miss" Rho Kloete, "Miss" Mandy Kelly, and "Miss" Elle Goering (with Grassland Community Mother's Day Out) for your heart!

And to Bailey, who's at my side even now, for always sticking with me.

Prologue

CHRISTMAS EVE, PRESENT DAY

Children are God's apostles, day by day
Sent forth to preach of love, and
hope, and peace.
— James Russell Lowell

It's snowing this afternoon. According to the forecasters we weren't supposed to have any snow on Christmas Eve, but the puffy white flakes that have been falling since morning have proven them wrong and it looks like we'll have a white Christmas after all. A snowplow makes its way through the center of town blowing huge white piles onto the side of the street. I pull out onto the road and drive in front of it, waving at the driver as I pass. I glance in my rearview mirror and see that two-year-old Mia is happy as she bounces a small Elmo doll up and down on the car seat. I turn up the radio and listen as Mel Torme sings "The

Christmas Song." Mia is squealing at Elmo. She has no idea what tomorrow is but she'll find out soon enough when her mom and dad take her out of her crib and show her the tree that will be swimming with gifts for her and her sister. I smile and turn the radio up louder. I drive through the town square and slow down as I pass three beautiful fir trees decorated with enormous green, red, and gold ornaments and magenta ribbon. Large, dazzling stars are perched on the top of the trees and they glitter in the sun. For as long as I can remember Norma Holt has decorated the trees. It started when she was a young woman in her twenties. She just took it upon herself to dress the trees each year when Christmas rolled around. That was long before there were formal city council meetings so no one opposed someone decorating city property. Somehow, over the years, no one ever objected as Norma worked her magic on the southwest corner of the city square. I never actually spoke with Norma, few people did. She was reclusive and chose to do her work alone but I would always pass, honk the horn, and she'd look up and wave. When Norma began her work it always seemed that the Christmas season had finally begun.

When I was a child it felt as if it took years for Christmas to arrive. The last few weeks would crawl by as I awaited the time to decorate the tree, bake cookies with my mom, and write out a detailed list for Santa. When the tree finally went up inside our family room and the lights on the outside of the house were hung I could barely contain the anticipation swelling inside me. Christmas was almost here! It was during those two to three weeks before Christmas that my brother, Richard, and I would draw a line in the sand and put all grievances aside. We couldn't run the risk of being found on Santa's naughty list. There were just too many gifts at stake. It seemed our home pulsed with happiness and joy during the time leading up to Christmas and I never wanted those feelings to end. No one could have told me then that those feelings would diminish as I got older or that Christmas would come around again in the blink of an eye or that I'd say things like, "It sure doesn't feel like Christmas this year." Somehow I got old and the wonder was lost.

I turn off the radio so I can hear Mia sing. She's attempting "Jingle Bells" but with the exception of "jingle" and "bells" I can't make out any other words. Her performance takes on a burlesque dimension as she grabs hold of her foot, raises her tiny leg, and belts out another chorus. "Where we going?" Mia asks when she catches me looking at her. She attempts to rise up out of the car seat to get a better look at where I'm driving. Mia has been in two foster homes in the past year. I don't know how many times I've heard little voices ask me questions from that backseat in my seventeen years as a social worker. How many times did I drop a child off at a foster family's home a few days before Christmas because his mother was arrested or put back into rehab? How many times have I taken a child back to his biological parent because his father met the goal set by the state and found a job and a place to live or his mother has a clean bill of health from the substance-abuse program she'd been in for the last four months? I've traveled these roads many times with tiny passengers just like Mia in my backseat asking where we were going.

I drive beneath a banner stretched across the street that reads Peace on Earth. There was a time, not so long ago that I could not imagine peace in my heart, let alone on earth. My joy was gone, happiness was a memory, and there was no reason to celebrate Christmas because there was no hope. At least that's what I thought. It wasn't always that way, though. Despite what happened, I had a happy childhood.

I was seven years old and my brother, Richard, was four when my father left. I saw hope drain from my mother. She was left with two small children and nowhere to live and no way to support them. I'd see her hunched over past-due bills on the kitchen table and tears would fill her eyes. There was no way to pay them. If there was a God it seemed He wasn't aware of my mother or her circumstances. "We'll just keep the faith," she'd tell me, repeating words she'd heard once in an old movie. But my problem was I didn't know what faith was so I had no idea how to keep something I didn't know about in the first place.

During that Christmas after my father left, my mother took Richard and me to church and we sat in the back row. "Hope came down dressed as a child," the minister said. "That Hope is the greatest gift the world has ever known."

I stood in my seat trying to see the child in the manger. How could a child come dressed as Hope?

"This child taught us how to love and forgive."

I strained to see the squirming baby. How in the world could a child teach anybody how to love and forgive?

"God can use anybody or anything," the minister said. "Don't ever underestimate who or what He'll use to get something done. But the choice to believe that is always yours to make."

I didn't understand what he meant about choosing to believe at the time but I would eventually and so would my own child. Years later, however, after my son was grown I would no longer believe. It was too painful. So I walked away.

For some reason I had always assumed that when God wanted our attention He would do something big that would rouse us from our sleep to bring us back to Him but I was wrong. God is always speaking. We are the ones who are hard of hearing. God is always patient, waiting for us to believe. We are the impatient ones, demanding to be convinced. We want something real, something we can touch and see to help us believe. The mountains, oceans, and skies aren't enough. Our babies who smile and laugh and reach for us aren't enough. We need more. And we have it, all around us, every day. If we would just take the time to listen and see we would walk toward God and believe, or at least some of us will. Some like me.

Although this is my story, it may be similar to yours. I still haven't filled in all the gaps. Perhaps I never will. But I have met many people along the way who have helped me put the pieces together; people who helped me to believe and hope again. At one time I said there was no hope but now I know that Hope is alive.

It just took me a few years to believe that.

One

ONE YEAR EARLIER

If you lose hope, somehow you lose the vitality that keeps life moving, you lose that courage to be, that quality that helps you go on in spite of it all. And so today I still have a dream.

— Martin Luther King Jr.

I jolted awake when I heard the snowplow outside my bedroom window. It snowed on December 17 and four days later it still hadn't taken a break. City workers were getting lots of overtime trying to get the roads passable for each workday. I looked at my clock: three-thirty. I'd probably never get back to sleep now. For years I could always sleep through the night but it had been close to four years since I had a full night's rest; if I awakened at three or four in the morning I was up for the rest of the day.

I threw my arm over my head and concentrated on falling back to sleep. I heard my husband, Mark, turn the shower on in the bathroom down the hall. He'd leave the house at four-thirty and be gone for the rest of the day. Our dog, Girl, pressed her nose to the bottom of the door; she wanted to be out with Mark but I was too tired to get up and open the door. After watching the closed door for several minutes she walked across the room and lay down on her pillow. At 4:00 A.M. I heard Mark walk down the stairs into the kitchen. He grabbed a bagel and poured a cup of coffee into an insulated mug before leaving the house. He didn't open the bedroom door to see if I might be awake or leave a note; he never did. I knew his schedule; he'd be home tomorrow morning after his flight. He'd had the same overnight flight for years. When I got up at four-thirty the kitchen was spotless; no signs of bagel crumbs or a knife crusted with cream cheese. It's the way I liked things. If his towel hadn't been wet in the bathroom I never would have known that Mark had even been in the house.

I turned the shower on and stepped inside, turning my face into the water. Four days until Christmas. I put my hands on my face and let the water wash over them. Why was the holiday season so long? I shook my head and washed my hair. After leaving work today I would have the next ten days off for Christmas. What in the world would I do with all that time? I sprayed the shower walls with cleaner and used a squeegee to remove the water from the glass doors before reaching for my towel.

By 5:30 A.M. I was dressed and ready for the day. The phone rang and I sighed. I knew who it was. "Hello."

"Good morning," my mother said.

"Mom, why do you call so early in the morning?"

"I knew you'd be up."

"But I could have been sleeping."

"Were you sleeping?"

"No."

"See. I knew you'd be up."

It was no use. I could always count on at least three or four early-morning calls a week. For years I had tried to break her from calling so early, with no success.

"Just wanted to let you know that I'm going Christmas shopping with Miriam today. What do you and Mark want for Christmas?"

I opened e-mail on my computer and half listened to her as I read through them.

"Do you need anything for the house?"

"We don't need anything, Mom."

"You may not need anything but you might *want* something! Do you want anything fun?" Every year she tried so hard.

"I can't think of anything."

She was quiet for a moment before sounding upbeat again. "Okay, well, if you think of anything you just let me know. I'll be out shopping on other days, too, and I can pick up whatever. You just let me —"

I cut her off and told her I'd call after I got home from work, and hung up.

When my father left, he told my mom he was going to the store to buy a newspaper and never came home. My mother had never known about the gambling; he was good at hiding things. He left right before the bottom dropped out. The police showed up on our doorstep before my mother had a chance to report him missing. He had taken thousands of dollars from the company he worked for and they had come to collect and throw him in jail (or in the case of his absence, take my mother to jail to question her or, as she said, scare the daylights out of her). I don't think the police believed her when she said she didn't know where my father was but they let her go.

We were evicted from our apartment, our belongings were seized, and the Dodge Dart was repossessed. We stayed in a motel for three nights, but then what little money my mother had ran out. We had been to church on occasion up to that point and on the morning we left the motel my mother packed our clothes in a paper bag and stuck it under her arm. She took hold of Richard's hand and instructed me to hold on to his as we made our way down the street. After walking several blocks Richard declared he was too tired to go any farther and my mother lifted him onto her hip and pulled me close to her side. "Stay right here beside me," she said, adjusting Richard and the paper bag.

"Where we going?" Richard asked over and over again. I never said a word. Somehow I knew not to say anything.

"We're going to see some people," my mother said. We walked across town and I could see the church in the distance. My mother hoisted Richard onto her other hip and handed me the paper bag to carry the rest of the way.

"It's too heavy," I said, regretting the words as soon as I said them. Mom took the bag from me and lugged it on her other side. When we got to the sidewalk leading up to the front door of the church my mother set Richard down and straightened his clothes.

"We going to church, Mommy?" Richard asked. "It's not Sunday."

My mother opened the door and looked around.

"What you looking for, Mommy?" Richard asked.

I rolled my eyes and wished he would be quiet for once.

"You looking for the church?"

"We're in the church," I said, hoping to ease the pressure off my mother. A woman in a pale pink dress peeked her head around the corner.

"Hi," she said, stepping toward us. "I thought I heard voices. Can I help you?" I looked up at my mother but she couldn't speak. Nothing was coming out. I noticed her eyes were filling with tears and the woman in pink noticed, too. She leaned down to Richard and me. "We've got a plateful of peanut butter cookies back in the kitchen that I made for a luncheon today." She leaned close and whispered. "Would you like some with a great big glass of milk?" We nodded and she took our hands. "I'm going to let your mother sit down here in the office while you two eat some cookies and play with all the toys we've got back there."

Another woman behind a desk with glasses

looked up and smiled at us. "Mrs. Burke," the woman in pink said. "These children are hungry for cookies. Maybe you and Pastor Burke might like to visit with their mother."

Mrs. Burke saw the tears in my mother's eyes and got up from her desk. "Just take your time," Mrs. Burke said to the woman in pink. "I've even got some chicken salad back there in the refrigerator if you want some of that." The thought of eating chicken salad at ten o'clock in the morning was less than appealing to me but Richard cheered with excitement.

I'm not sure how many cookies we ate but when Mom walked into the kitchen the plate was nearly empty. "Thank you," my mother said, looking at the woman in pink. "Thank you very much."

We walked outside and a woman driving a station wagon was in the driveway waving at us. "I'm Geraldine Culberson," she said, looking at my mother. "Just hop on in." Mom ushered us inside the car and Geraldine drove us to her home. "We've got a bed and a couch down here," she said, leading us into the basement. "You can put your clothes in here," she said, resting her hand on a small chest of drawers, "and the bathroom is right at the top of the stairs."

She turned to leave. "I'll have lunch ready in about an hour, so you just get settled in and come on up whenever you're ready."

My mother sat on the edge of the bed. She didn't say anything; she just pulled Richard and me close to her and cried.

We lived in Geraldine and George's basement for six months until someone else in the church had a small apartment we could rent. Before long, church members dropped off a small black-and-white TV set, a full-size refrigerator, sofa, beds, toys, and clothes. Mom found a part-time job answering phones and doing the books for a small dress shop while Geraldine watched Richard. When I got out of school I walked to the Culbersons' house and when Mom was finished working we all walked home to our apartment together. At night I would watch my mother go through the bills my father had left and I always saw the same look on her face. There was no way out.

My mother lost her smile after my father left. I was too young to fully realize what was wrong but knew it had to have something to do with the mess my father had left us in. Creditors were threatening her on every side but she had nothing left for them to take. She'd write a check for five or ten dollars and stick it in an envelope hoping that her attempts to pay off the debts would prove something to the creditors. For some it did but for most it didn't. It was a few weeks before Christmas when my mother broke down at the kitchen table. She held on to several letters and wept. I ran down the street for Mrs. Culberson. She read through a letter and patted my mother's shoulder. "Nobody's going to take your kids away from you, Charlotte," she said. "Don't you worry about that!"

Several days later Pastor and Mrs. Burke knocked on the apartment door. My mother invited them in and put a pot of coffee on to brew. When she finished her coffee Mrs. Burke opened her purse and pulled out an envelope. She pushed it across the table to my mother. Mom opened it and gasped. "I can't take this," she whispered.

"You take it and pay off every single bill," Pastor Burke said.

"But there's more here than what we owe." My mother moved the envelope back across the table but Mrs. Burke stopped her. "I can't take it." Mrs. Burke put the envelope in Mom's hand.

"I can't go back to all these people and tell them that what God laid on their heart was wrong. God wanted them to help and that's what they've done."

Mom sat clutching the fat envelope. "But I don't know who gave this," she whispered. "How can I ever thank them?"

"They didn't do it for the thanks, Charlotte," Mrs. Burke said. "But God knows who they are. He'll thank them."

Mom shook her head and used a towel sitting on the table to wipe her face. Mrs. Burke leaned toward Mom and squeezed her hand. "Sometimes we're not supposed to be in on every single part of God's plan. Sometimes we just need to take the blessing and run."

We would never know who gave us the money. When adults would speak to my mother at church I'd listen for some clue they might give to help us clear up the puzzle. But no one ever acted as if they knew anything. Tears ran down my mother's face as she wrapped her arms around Mrs. Burke's neck. The Burkes quietly left and I watched from the hallway as my mother cried, clutching the envelope. That was the end of the creditors, the letters, and the threats . . . and the return of my mother's smile.

For several Christmases leading up to that one I would, under the guise of "cleaning," rummage through my mother's closet or beneath her bed in an attempt to find even the smallest gift. "Patricia, Christmas isn't all about you," Mom said one day, ushering me out of her room. "It's not about what you can get. It's about what you can give." At the time that notion seemed crazy to me but after my mother received the envelope full of money from a church full of strangers I knew exactly what she meant.

I poured what coffee there was left in my cup down the sink, cleaned and polished the coffeepot, turned it on an angle so it sat just so on the counter, and opened the garage door. I wanted to beat the traffic that would be traveling across town so I left an hour early for my first appointment. It took me forty minutes and when I pulled into the drive I noticed that the Lymans had decorated the outside of their house and trees with lights. Santa and his sleigh were perched on top of the roof close to the chimney and Frosty or some snowman that looked like him greeted visitors at the front door. I opened my trunk and waited for Justin. Claire Lyman opened the door and waved, placing her hand on Justin's shoulder as they walked down the front steps. "How are you, Patricia?" Claire asked.

"I'm great," I said. "How's everybody in the Lyman family?"

She gave me a big okay sign and I reached for Justin's suitcase. "How are you, Justin?" He shrugged his shoulders. Justin placed his plain brown suitcase inside the trunk. "The house looks great, Claire."

Claire put her arm around Justin. "Justin helped us. We couldn't have done it without him."

"Wow Justin! This place looks awesome."

He looked at the ground and Claire caught my eye. She wrapped her arms around Justin's small shoulders and kissed his face. "Thanks for staying with us, Justin."

He nodded but didn't take his eyes off the ground. He didn't want to leave. "Can I ever come back?" His voice was quiet.

Claire kept her arm around him and looked at me. She turned him toward her and made him look at her. "You and your mother can come by anytime," she said. It wasn't what Justin wanted to hear.

"Can I come back to stay?"

"We love you, Justin, but your mom loves you very much and she needs you."

She opened the door of the car and Justin slunk into the passenger seat.

"Oh, wait!" Claire said, running into the house. She ran back to the car carrying a package wrapped in bright Christmas paper. "You can't open this until Christmas," she said, placing the gift on the boy's lap. "It's for you and your mom." She looked at me and smiled, and I got behind the wheel, waving at her. I had worked with Claire and her husband for several years now. They were foster parents I could always depend on and were willing to open their home to any child. I backed out of the driveway and noticed Claire waving at Justin. He wouldn't look up.

"Claire's waving, Justin." I stopped at the end of the driveway for a moment to give him time to respond. He didn't. She continued to wave. I pulled onto the road. "Justin, Claire's waving at you." He pressed his hands into his thighs. As I drove past their mailbox and front of the house Justin spun in his seat to catch the last glimpse of Claire. He threw his hand in the back window and waved till we rounded the corner. He clutched the gift and slumped back in the seat. At twelve, Justin had been in and out of foster homes since he was eight years old. It was always hard to leave the ones where he felt he was loved. In the past nine months he had been in two separate foster homes as his mother went through rehab. I knew he didn't want to go back and live with his mother again.

"Your mom sure is excited to see you," I

said, turning my head to catch a glimpse of him.

He looked out the window and didn't say anything.

"She said she's going to wait for you to get home and then you both can go pick out a Christmas tree this weekend."

He remained content to look out the window. I knew what he was thinking but I also knew he was wrong . . . at least I hoped he was wrong.

I pulled into a grocery store parking lot and turned toward him. I'd seen lots of parents come out of rehab and many times I knew that they'd fall back into the traps they weren't strong enough to resist. But other times I knew when they were genuinely clean and wanted to get their life back in order. They no longer said things they knew I wanted to hear but talked to me from a broken heart. I knew Justin's mom wanted her son and her life back. "She's met every goal set by the state and she's clean, Justin. And she's going to stay clean."

"Yeah, right," he said, mumbling, turning toward the window again.

"Your mom has changed, Justin."

He didn't say anything but watched a man load groceries into the back of his SUV.

I pulled his face toward me. "Your mom

is not the same person that you remember."

His eyes welled up with tears. "She always says she's going to change but she never does." He slung the tears from his face, embarrassed. "She always promises that she'll be different but she never is. She just lies to get people to think she's different!" He ran his coat sleeve under his nose.

I reached for a tissue out of the glove compartment and handed it to him, pulling him onto my shoulder. "She has changed," I whispered. "I know it's hard for you to believe but I've seen her and talked with her and she's a different person now."

He shook his head. He couldn't believe it.

"She found a job."

"She won't be able to keep it."

I squeezed him closer to me. "She'll be cutting hair again and she loves to do that. She was working in a factory before and she didn't like that."

"She couldn't cut hair before because everybody always fired her."

I turned his face toward me. "I know this is hard." A single tear ran down his cheek. "But your mom loves you so much. She's worked hard to get clean, Justin, and she wants you back to stay. I know it'll be easy to act angry toward her but that's not going to help her or you."

He nodded.

"I've worked with a lot of people over the years and I *know* that your mom loves you very much."

He fumbled with the package in his hands. "Will you come to our apartment a lot?"

"I'll have to make my appointed visits, yes."

"Will you come over even if you don't have an appointed visit?"

I smiled. "Will you be able to provide some sort of liquid refreshment? Perhaps a soda or iced tea?"

"Okay."

"How about a confection of some sort?"

"I guess so but I don't know what a confection is."

I laughed and put on my seat belt. "Well, you better find out, because I will need a confection of the chocolate persuasion!"

When we arrived at the apartment complex I put my hand on Justin's shoulder and walked him up the two flights of stairs. Rita Ramirez opened the door before I could knock, and pulled her son to her, burying her face in the top of his head. She was only thirty but looked ten years older. She spoke in rapid-fire Spanish and I put up my hands.

"No fair," I said. "English only. For all I know you're criticizing my outfit or my hair and that would just ruin the rest of my day."

Rita stood back and looked at Justin. "You're so handsome," she said, holding his face. "Are you hungry?"

He shook his head.

"Miss Patricia, are you hungry?" She held on to Justin's hand and led us into the small kitchen. "Would you like some coffee?" She poured me a cup and we sat down together at the table. I had looked through Rita's apartment and gone over the expectations of the Department of Family Services with her on an earlier date so there was nothing left to do except wish them well.

I finished my coffee and stood to leave. "I'll let you know when I'll be back," I said, opening the door.

"You can come by anytime for a confection, though," Justin said, reminding me to come visit.

"I just might do that," I said, looking in his eyes that held so much doubt.

Rita grabbed my arm before I walked out the door. "Thank you, Miss Patricia. Thank you for bringing my Justin back to me."

I smiled at them, another one of my fragile families trying to start over again. Rita wrapped her arms around me. "I hope you have a beautiful Christmas!" I couldn't say anything but waved as I walked toward the stairs and whispered a prayer that this time Rita would make it.

The day before I had typed Rita's address onto the front of an envelope and used it as the return address as well. Enclosed were two gift certificates: one for a hardware store where she and Justin could find Christmas decorations and one for a nearby grocery store. They'd receive it in the mail by tomorrow at the latest. It wasn't as much as what my mother had received in the envelope so many years ago but I hoped it was enough to help Rita and Justin have an extraordinary Christmas together.

I drove through Knight's Auto Wash before heading to the office. I didn't want salt buildup underneath, and Justin had left a trail of mud and dirt from his boots. I instructed the employees to move the seats back in order to clean well under them. They hadn't done that last week. Once the car was clean, I drove to the office, turned on the computer at my desk, and rummaged through the Ramirez file, making sure it was updated. Weeks earlier many of the office staff had taken the last two hours of the day to decorate a small Christmas tree and hang ivy throughout the office. I made sure I had an appointment at that time so I could avoid the Christmas cheer and banter. Christmas was no longer a time of joy for me and I didn't want to put a damper on the staff's festivities.

I closed a drawer in my desk and the sound made a toy fish on Roy Braeden's desk move to the tune of "Grandma Got Run Over by a Reindeer." I shook my head. For the last few weeks that fish had been driving me crazy. Thankfully, the dancing Santa was broken this year, although Roy picked him up every day trying to diagnose the problem. Roy had worked for family services longer than I had. His first wife died after twenty-eight years of marriage, leaving Roy lonely and depressed. Thinking he was in love, Roy married Ella a year after his wife's funeral. It was a mistake. Roy realized he wasn't in love but just desperate for companionship. The marriage lasted less than two years. Now he'd been dating Barbara for four years but was gun-shy about marriage although I often told him that he was going to lose Barbara if he didn't marry her. She was a good woman and Roy was a good man. "You're good for each other," I said time and again to him. Roy was a father of four, grandfather of five and counting, and a good friend. I noticed a doughnut sitting on his desk across the aisle from me and I rolled over in my chair and swiped it, taking a bite. I didn't think of it as stealing. I thought of it as doing him a favor. His cholesterol was up and he had no business eating a greasy doughnut. I heard his voice and pushed the last of the doughnut into my mouth. He walked to his desk and stopped.

"Patti, did you see a doughnut on my desk?"

I leaned over to look toward his desk. "No, I don't see anything."

He opened a drawer and looked inside. "I could swear I put a doughnut right here." He started toward the lounge. "I'll just go get another one."

"There's none back there," I said, typing.

He threw up his hands. "All a man wants is a lousy doughnut to help him get through the day. Is that too much to ask?"

"From my view it looks like the man has had too many doughnuts over the years."

He stopped and looked at me. "I guess you went into social work so you could encourage and uplift."

I laughed as my phone rang.

"Do people say I'm heavy?" he asked, pulling his shirt across his belly.

I waved my hand to get him to be quiet and picked up the receiver. It was Lynn McSwain, our supervisor. He was calling from his cell phone.

"I may be beefy but beefy's good," Roy said. "Beefy's not heavy."

I turned my back to him and pressed the phone closer to my ear. "Okay," I said. "I'll take care of her." I hung up the phone. "Bridget Sloane was taken to County a few minutes ago," I said, pulling a file from my cabinet.

"What for?"

"Selling to an undercover cop. I have to place Mia." I shook my head, shoving files into my briefcase. "She left Mia in her crib at seven o'clock last night and never went back home." Roy looked down at his watch. "Fifteen and a half hours," I said, helping him do the math. "The police are at the apartment now." Bridget Sloane was eighteen years old and the mother of a beautiful ten-month-old daughter who was an albatross around Bridget's neck. Bridget had been on the move since she ran away from home at sixteen. If she had any idea who the father was she would have fought him for child support so she could use the money for drugs. But she didn't even know she was pregnant until she was three months along and by then she couldn't remember where she had been, who she had lived with, or what she had smoked. We had placed Mia in a foster home for three months when she was born so Bridget could finish a jail term for bad checks. I called that foster family again to see if they were available to take Mia this time. The message on their machine said they were out of town. I called Sandra and Guy Michaels, a new family I had worked with and liked.

"Bring her anytime," Sandra said. I hung up the phone and grabbed my purse. "You up for tagging along?" I asked Roy. He took his jacket off the coat rack and followed me to the elevator.

We entered Bridget's apartment and found a police officer bouncing Mia up and down. She was screaming. It was cold inside the tiny three-room apartment. "We're with DFS," I said to the officer. Reaching for Mia, I gave the officer my business card. "Doesn't the electricity work?" I asked.

"Nothing works," the officer said. "Guess the electric company turned it off."

I wrapped Mia's blanket around her and held her close. Her hands were freezing.

"She's been screaming since we got here," he said. "She's screamed so much that she threw up. We couldn't find any diapers so I made one out of paper towels."

I put my hand on Mia's bottom and felt

the massive "diaper" the officer had created.

"Shh, shh, shh," I whispered into Mia's ear. "It's okay, Mia. It's okay." She straightened her legs and screamed louder. I rummaged through the kitchen cabinets looking for formula.

"There's nothing here," the officer told me. "We've already looked."

"I'll pack her clothes," Roy said, walking toward Mia's bedroom.

The officer handed him a plastic grocery bag filled with clothes. "I knew you'd want them. They were the only clothes I could find."

Roy took them and looked in Mia's room at the mess that was in the portable crib. I walked behind him holding Mia.

"Looks like Bridget ran out of diapers a few days ago," Roy said. I shook my head and tried to quiet Mia's screams. She was starving and I had to find her something to eat. I headed for the door.

"What will happen to her?" the officer asked.

"She'll go into a foster home," I said.

"Will her mother get her back?"

"I don't know."

"No baby should ever have to go through what she did."

"I know," I said, bouncing Mia. Roy

opened the door and we walked down the hallway.

A woman stuck her head out of her apartment door. "Ma'am," she said. "Ma'am!"

I turned around and saw her coming toward me holding a bottle. "I heard the police talking to you." She handed me the bottle. "It's not formula but it's warm milk. Maybe it will help."

"Thank you," I said. "You wouldn't happen to have a diaper, would you?" She ran back into her apartment and carried out a handful.

"They'll be too big but they'll still work." She disappeared into her apartment and we could hear her bolt the door behind her. I handed the diapers to Roy and put the nipple of the bottle into Mia's mouth. She continued to scream and I ran the nipple over her lips and the inside of her mouth.

"Here you go, Mia," I said. "Here you go, sweet girl." She closed her lips around the nipple and began to suck. I wiped the tears off her face and kissed the top of her head, pulling her closer to me so she'd feel safe. "How about we get in the car and find you something to eat, huh?" Roy opened the rear car door and I laid Mia on the backseat of the car and pulled off the paper towel diaper. "Totally dry," I said to Roy. After fifteen and a half hours of being alone I was sure Mia was on her way to dehydration. I fastened a diaper on her, strapped her into the car seat, and started to cover her legs with her blanket but stopped. I smelled it and set it aside. It reeked of cigarette smoke. "Would you get the blanket out of the trunk?" I asked Roy. He popped the trunk and handed it to me. I tucked it around Mia, propping the bottle on it so she could continue to drink. "Food's coming up," I said, noticing the bottle was all but empty at this point. I knew as soon as it ran out that she'd be screaming again. I sat in the backseat with Mia as Roy drove to a small nearby diner.

I handed the waitress Mia's bottle and asked that she fill it with milk and warm it as quickly as possible. Mia began to cry again and I assured her that the bottle would be returning. "I'll never understand it, Roy."

He nodded. What I was thinking went without saying in our line of work.

"There are so many people who would love to take care of this baby."

"I'm sure somebody will," Roy said. I knew what he meant. Bridget would see a lengthy jail sentence this time for selling drugs and Mia would be placed in a foster home and then probably up for adoption. The waitress handed me the warm bottle and I stuck it back in Mia's mouth. She stopped screaming.

"She's loud but she's cute," the waitress said. "Your mommy's not going to let you starve," she said, talking to Mia. I didn't say anything. There was no point in explaining the situation.

Roy watched the waitress leave to fill our drink order. "Now, why did she think you were Mia's mother but she didn't think I was her dad?"

"Look at us, Roy," I said, patting Mia's back. "She knows a young chick like me would never marry an old rooster like you."

He stared at me. "There's another reason you're good for social work! You're so gentle and kind. You're what we like to call the inspiring sort."

I laughed. I always knew which buttons to push to aggravate Roy. The waitress brought the potatoes and a spoon and I held Mia in my lap to feed her.

"I'm sorry, Mia," I said. "I'm so sorry that you were scared." She had no idea what I was saying but was so excited to have food that she bounced up and down in my arms as I fed her each bite. Roy and I watched her eat for several minutes.

"I'm always amazed at how sweet they are," Roy said. "You'd think they'd be bitter but they somehow always manage to laugh." Roy tickled Mia's leg and she pulled it away from him, giggling.

"Year after year I keep thinking that things will change, but they don't."

Roy threw his arms in the air. "You keep thinking what will change? People? You think everybody's going to wake up one day and do the right thing? That they'll suddenly take care of their children or stop selling drugs? Things like that are never going to change as long as there are people on this planet."

I put the bottle in Mia's mouth. "Does your tummy feel better now, Mia?" I asked, setting her onto the table. "Huh? Does your tummy feel better?" I'm not sure what I said but she laughed at me. "Was that funny?" She flapped her arms and squealed. "If you think that's funny you should see me when I'm really on," I said, picking her up. "I can bring the house down." She laughed again and tried to put the bottle back into her mouth. I motioned for the waitress to bring more milk. Roy filled the bottle and handed it to me. I guided it into Mia's mouth and she went heavy in my arms, content to rest there for the remainder of the day.

"See, I told you your mommy wouldn't let you starve," the waitress said, squeezing Mia's leg as we stood to leave. I thanked the waitress and wrapped the blanket around Mia as we left the restaurant.

We drove to Guy and Sandra Michaels' house and left Mia with Sandra. I went back to the office to file my report. At the end of the day I could hear everyone talking about their Christmas plans. I kept working, hoping they would leave me out of all the "Are you staying in town or going away for Christmas" conversations, and they did. Throughout the years the office staff knew to leave me alone. Everyone, that is, except Roy.

"Is Mark working on Christmas, Patti?"

I sighed. I knew I couldn't escape it. Roy had asked me to spend Christmas with his family for the last three years but each time I declined.

"I don't know."

He knew I was lying. Mark had worked the last two Christmases. Why would this one be any different?

"When you find out, let me know. Barbara's coming over. All the kids and grandkids, too. Everybody would love to see you. Barbara's bringing over a huge bird. We'll have plenty of food to go around."

I gathered my things and handed Roy a small gift I had wrapped for him, a leather journal with his name engraved on it.

"I didn't get you anything," he said, sounding more frustrated than grateful.

"I don't need anything," I said, putting on my coat. I hugged Roy good-bye before he had a chance to open the gift. "Have a great Christmas." I headed for the elevator doors so I could make a quick getaway. I drove home, entered our empty house alone, closed the door, and tried to imagine how anyone could look forward to the holidays.

Two

Hope never abandons you;
you abandon it.
— George Weinberg

I'd been home less than thirty minutes. I barely had time to change my clothes and sort through the mail when the phone rang. I looked at my watch — six o'clock. Right on time. I never actually had to call my mother because she would always call me before I got the chance to get to the phone.
"Hello."

"How was your day, Patti?"

"It was great!" I always told her my days were great.

"What are you eating tonight?"

"I haven't even opened the fridge to see what's in there," I said.

"Then come on over. I've got chicken in the oven and there's too much here for just the two of us." My mother married Lester Allen when I was fourteen. He was a member of the church that had been so kind to us, never married, and worked as a construction supervisor. When he and my mother began sitting together at church I didn't think anything of it; but when he started to join us for Sunday lunch at our house I became suspicious and confused. Lester was stocky with a round face and glasses and his pants were always about an inch too short. I never imagined that my mother would find him attractive; I didn't. But after they began dating I knew why my mother liked Lester. He was good to her. He was helpful and kind and could always make her laugh. He respected her and that respect carried over to Richard and me. Looking back, I don't know why he would want to marry a woman with one teenager and another teen in the making; I think most men would run away from that sort of commitment, but Lester was different. He never tried to swoop in and pretend he was our father; he knew he wasn't but he quickly became a father to us, doing everything a dad did and what our own father never had. Richard loved Lester from the beginning. I never realized it, although I'm sure my mother did, but Richard was desperate for a man in his life. Shortly after Les and Mom married, we went to the courthouse and Lester adopted us. Soon after, Richard began calling him Dad. I thought it would sound strange to call Lester that but when I tried it at sixteen it felt comfortable and safe. He'd been Dad ever since.

Although I was tired I drove to Mom and Dad's house. I hadn't spent much time with them lately and I knew my absence was concerning them. After the meal I stood to clear the plates. "Does Mark get in tonight?" Mom asked. She knew he didn't; she just wanted to bring him up to see how he was doing.

"Tomorrow morning," I said.

"Poor guy. He must be so tired after those overnight flights."

"He's used to them," I said.

Mom pushed all the scraps down the garbage disposal and turned it on. "I found him a back massager today for Christmas," she said, talking over the grinding of the disposal. "It's got a long handle so he can get to his lower back." She used a spatula and held it over her shoulder and down her back to demonstrate. "Do you think he'll like that?"

I loaded dishes into the dishwasher. "He'll

love it." There was no point in telling her again that she didn't have to get us anything; actually that we would *prefer* that she didn't. Regardless of what happened, she thought of Mark as a son and wasn't about to let Christmas roll around without wrapping presents for him.

Mom liked Mark the moment I brought him home from college for Thanksgiving vacation. She had never come out and said anything about the other boys I had dated but I always knew when she didn't like one of them. "Is he watching cartoons?" she asked one Saturday morning, looking into the living room at my boyfriend who had taken food out of the kitchen and was eating cornflakes on the sofa.

"Yes," I said, hoping she wouldn't say anything else.

"I didn't realize eighteen-year-old men watched cartoons." That's all she had to say.

And on a separate occasion she looked at her watch when another boyfriend visited. "It's already eight-thirty. I'd start the pancakes but I don't know how much longer he'll sleep." When he walked into the kitchen at nine-fifteen with messy hair, a ratty T-shirt and boxer shorts, I saw the look on her face and hoped she wouldn't say anything. She didn't.

"Ambition never hurt anyone," she'd tell me over and over. "You'll never find a bum with ambition." That was my mother's favorite word when I was dating: "bum." "Don't marry a bum," she'd say. I knew she thought my biological father was a bum but she never said it, at least not to me. "Bums are a dime a dozen. They're easy to find. But there are some good men out there, too. They might be harder to find but they're out there."

Mark was different. He wasn't a bum. He called my mom and dad "Mr. and Mrs. Allen," he awoke early and always made his bed, he never took food out of the kitchen, and he was "ambitious." My mother loved seeing that in young people. When Mark opened the car door for me I could see my mother's face light up. Mark knew what he wanted to do with his life and Mom could tell that he wanted me as part of that life. She knew he loved me.

I met him in the middle of my sophomore year. I was standing in line behind him in the cafeteria when he turned to grab a glass. His hand knocked my tray to the floor and spaghetti sauce splattered us both. "I am so sorry," he said, brushing aside goopy, wet spaghetti noodles that hung from my brown suede purse. I looked at him and blushed.

He was on the football team; I'd seen him play but had never spoken to him.

"It's no big deal," I said, pressing a wad of napkins against my skirt. He was busy wiping the bright red sauce off the floor. When he stood to throw away the mess of napkins in his hand he looked at me for the first time and stopped. He had dark blond hair, brown eyes, and the sweetest smile. He held his gaze and I looked at the floor, wondering why I couldn't have been wearing something cuter.

"I'm an idiot," he said. "I'm really sorry." He grabbed another tray and tried to hand it to me. "Let me help you."

"No, no. I'll just go clean up and then try again . . . when it's safer to come back." I hoped with everything that was in me that he would say he'd wait for me so we could eat together.

"Can I wait for you?" he asked. He wasn't cocky. He wasn't so sure of himself that he *knew* I'd want to eat with him but actually questioned whether *I* would want to eat with him.

I felt my heart jump, and nodded.

Mark got his pilot's license when he was seventeen. During the summers he worked for a small air cargo service, first in the warehouse, then the office, and finally flying deliveries for them. When he graduated he planned to move out of state and work for a commercial airline. Mark was a year ahead of me in college and the thought of being separated a year didn't appeal to either one of us so when he graduated we married. My mother would have preferred that I finish college and I assured her that I would once Mark and I were settled. But I got pregnant quicker than we anticipated. Eleven months after we married I gave birth to Sean and a month later I received my degree. Sean looked like me but had his dad's disposition. I could take him anywhere and he was content, unlike me. I was always looking for something to do. I soon discovered that once Sean was born I had plenty to do!

It's funny how excited you are when you learn you're going to have a baby but then dread so many things that come with that new life: things like the first steps, because you realize you won't have as much cuddle time now that the baby has discovered he has legs; the day he wants to dress himself because he's "a big boy now"; the time he stops calling the Fairy Godmother "Mary Godmother"; the day he realizes there's a "th" on the word "think" and he no longer says, "I fink so"; the day he boards the bus for kindergarten, or the day the finger paintings of blobs that he swears is a rainbow or lion or mommy and daddy come down off the refrigerator door. While parents share joy with their child in these events, there's a little piece of their heart that aches. Someone once told me that when you become a parent you wear your heart on your sleeve for the next eighteen years of your life.

"Oh, that's ridiculous," my mother said when I shared it with her. "You don't wear your heart on your sleeve for the next eighteen years . . . you wear it there for the rest of your life."

When Sean was fourteen months old Mark was offered a job with another air cargo airline closer to our parents. My mother was ecstatic when she discovered we would be living, as she would say, "twenty minutes from her front door." We tried to get pregnant when Sean was two but after two unsuccessful years we knew there was a problem. As Sean got older and closer to kindergarten it seemed that we weren't meant to have any other children. I went to work when Sean started school, but I never got pregnant again, although we never closed that door. "It's okay," Mark said. "This is our family and I'm happy."

For years we did have a happy household, though there was stress. The airline Mark worked for went bankrupt, leaving thousands of employees without jobs, Mark's mother was diagnosed with breast cancer and went through years of treatments, and Mark and I could always find reason to argue over finances (he could always buy on impulse but I had to mull things over before buying a new car or piece of stereo equipment). Once while riding in his car seat Sean listened as Mark and I got into a heated argument over money. "Mommy. Daddy. Be friends," he said, trying to pull himself toward us. He was two and a half years old and full of wisdom.

When Sean ran through the front door after his first day of kindergarten, he said, "I'm never leaving you, Mommy. I'm staying with you forever."

"But what will you do when you marry a beautiful girl?"

"Live here," he said.

"But she'll need you to help take care of your house and she'll want you to live there because she loves you."

"But I'll love *you,*" he said. "Always, always, always."

I kept my great-grandfather's pocket watch on display in our bedroom. It hung from a hook on the tarnished brass holder he had given my grandfather when he passed it down to him. When I wasn't looking, Sean would open the drawers of the dresser and climb up to the watch, slipping it into his pocket. "This watch is very special to Mommy," I'd say, taking it out of his hands. "We need to take good care of it."

He'd nod and pretend to listen but days later I'd find him in his room playing with the watch.

"You can have this when you're older," I'd say. "My great-grandmother gave it to my great-grandfather one year when they were very young. Then he gave it to my grandfather when he grew up, and he gave it to your grandmother, and Grandma gave it to me. So you're the next one who's going to get to take care of it." That story never appealed to Sean's young mind so I finally moved the watch to the den and set it high on the bookshelf far from his reach.

When Sean was older we always opened our home to his friends because we'd much rather have them in our home rather than send Sean to a home where we didn't know anything about the parents. Like all teenagers, he and his friends could be rambunctious. They were wrestling in the den one afternoon when Sean was slammed into the bookshelf. My great-grandfather's pocket watch crashed to the floor and Sean's knee fell on top of it, crushing it beyond repair. I was distraught over his carelessness and lack of respect.

"I'm sorry, Mom. I'll buy you another one," he said.

"Don't be flippant, Sean," I said in front of his friends. "You can't replace a family heirloom and the memories attached to it." I picked up the broken pieces of the watch and looked over my shoulder. "Your friends need to go home right now and don't plan to do anything with them for the next month."

Looking back, I know I was too harsh on him but at the time I was sad over the loss yet also angry and my emotions got in the way. I kept the shattered watch in a box for the longest time hoping an expert watch repairman would be able to help, but as I'd suspected, the watch was ruined. I eventually threw everything away and Sean repeated again that he would replace it someday. "It doesn't matter," I said, kissing him months later. "It's just a thing."

For his senior prom, Mark and I took pictures of Sean and his date in our backyard. He looked so handsome in his black tux and she was adorable in a foam green shimmering dress. We walked them to the car and watched as Sean let her in the passenger side. He walked by us and leaned in to me. "Always," he whispered, making me cry.

Those days seemed so far away now. It was then, when we were young and everything was new that we were all happy. But life gets in the way, circumstances change, and despite our hope that it will never happen to us, happiness fades.

I washed the last pan and rinsed it, setting it in the dish drainer for my mother to dry. "Thanks for dinner, Mom. I better head home."

Mom took the pan and dried it, placing it inside the cabinet beneath the stove. "Have you and Mark heard about the live Nativity they're doing out at Longworth Farm? They've got food and caroling and they're even giving sleigh rides."

"I think I read about that in the paper," I said, putting on my coat.

"Les and I are going to go one night. Why don't the two of you come with us?"

"I might be able to go but I'm not sure if Mark's going to be around."

She wrung the dish towel between her hands. "It'd be nice if both of you could go," Dad said.

I was quiet. I didn't want to get into this

conversation with them again. I moved toward my purse.

"Patti, there are so many counselors who could help," Mom said.

I held up my hand. "We've tried counselors, Mom. No, they can't help." I moved toward the door and opened it.

"Patti, Mark loves you and I know you love him. Please don't let this happen. Please do everything you can before you —"

I cut her off. "I have done everything I can, Mom," I said, defeated. "We've both done everything we can."

In the last several days Mark had gone through his closet and begun to pack his things into boxes and suitcases. I know Mom had seen the boxes and I know she wondered why I hadn't tried to stop Mark but I couldn't. I didn't know how. In four years I hadn't given him any reason to stay. I was surprised he stayed as long as he did. But what Mom and Dad didn't know is that I had asked Mark about the bags a few days earlier when I saw him cleaning out his closet. "Are you leaving, Mark?"

He put his hands in his pockets and stared at the floor. "I can't live like this, Patricia." He was leaving. "I don't know what to do anymore."

I walked out of the room. It was a hopeless solution but Mark and I had both known for the last year that it was the only thing left to do. Soon there wouldn't be anything left of this family.

"But you're acting like it's over," Mom said. "There's always hope, Patti. All you —"

I put up my hand. "Stop it, Mom. Just stop." I saw the look in her eyes as I closed the door behind me and I knew I'd hurt her. I got in the car and felt myself shaking. How had I become so cold? I should have stayed and talked with them but I was tired in every way so I drove home, went to bed, and prayed for just one day of peace in my life.

THREE

We have to go into the despair and go beyond it, by working and doing for somebody else, by using it for something else.

— Elie Wiesel

I was dreaming. I don't know how many times the phone rang before I realized what was happening. It was almost midnight. "Patricia, this is Karen Delphy. I'm sorry to call you so late but I have an emergency."

"What is it?"

"We just received word from Eric's mother that his father has taken a turn for the worse." I knew Eric's father had battled emphysema for the last several years. "Doctors have said that if family wants to see him one last time that they need to come now."

"I understand. I'll come get Emily right

away." Five-year-old Emily Weist had been in Karen and Eric's home for the past five months. I'd try to call another foster family on my way to pick up Emily.

I had first met Emily five months earlier in July. I was able to piece together her story from what she and her neighbor, Greta Larson, told me. On that July day Emily sat on the bathroom counter and watched her mother get ready for work. "I'm going to call Mrs. Larson to see if she can watch you tonight," her mother said. Sixty-one-year-old Greta lived down the street from the tiny duplex Tracy and Emily rented and had always been kind to them. She would often bring meals for them to eat, drop off a winter coat or pair of shoes for Emily, or watch Emily when Tracy was unexpectedly called in to work a shift for someone at the restaurant.

The doorbell rang and Emily jumped off the counter.

"I'll get it." She opened the door and found Greta holding a bowl covered with aluminum foil. "Miss Greta," Emily said, throwing herself into Greta's legs.

"Have you eaten?" Greta asked.

"Nope."

"How does chicken pot pie sound?"

"Yum-mee," the little girl said, taking the bowl from her. She set it down on the red, white, and blue plastic tablecloth covered with fireworks.

"It's left over from yesterday but it's still good. I had it for lunch."

Tracy walked out of the bathroom brushing her hair. "Hi, Greta, I was just going to call you." She stopped when she saw that Greta was wearing nice slacks and a blouse. "Wow. You look so nice."

"It's our anniversary and Hal is taking me out for dinner tonight."

Emily snapped her head to look at Greta. "So you won't be able to watch . . ." Tracy moved toward Emily to quiet her.

Greta looked at Emily's face and realized something was wrong. "Are you working tonight, Tracy? Do you need me to watch Emily?"

"No. You and Hal go out and have a great anniversary."

"We can do it another night. It's no big deal. We've had forty-one other anniversaries."

"No. I can find someone else."

Greta didn't believe her. "Are you sure?"

"Positive."

For as long as Greta had known Tracy she'd never seen anyone else take care of Emily.

"Why don't Hal and I just bring Emily with us?"

"Yeah!" Emily shrieked.

"No," Tracy said, leading Greta out. "Have a great time and thanks for the food. I'm calling someone right now to come be with Emily."

"Call me if you can't find anyone," Greta said, walking down the driveway. Tracy picked up the phone and started to dial a number. No one was home. She dialed another number and it had been disconnected. Twenty minutes later she was out of phone numbers and at risk of being late for work. She threw on her uniform and sat down at the kitchen table as Emily finished her meal. She put her head down to think.

"What's wrong, Mom?" Emily asked. Tracy groaned and rolled her head back and forth on her arms.

She lifted her head and looked at Emily. "Listen to me," she said, buttoning her uniform. She took the clock down from the wall. "I have to be at work when the big hand is on the twelve and the little hand is on the six." She moved the hands of the clock to show Emily. "It'll look like this when I start my shift. I want you to go to bed when the little hand is on the eight and the big hand is on the six." She turned the clock to show Emily what it would look like. "Okay?"

The little girl nodded.

"I get off work when the little hand is on the ten and the big hand is on the twelve but you'll be asleep by then anyway." She picked up the clock and took the batteries out. "I'm going to set this for eight-thirty so you know what it looks like. Keep watching the clock in the living room and when it looks just like this go to bed."

Emily stopped eating and looked at her mom. "Who's going to watch me?"

Tracy sighed. Emily hadn't understood. "You're going to have to stay here by yourself tonight, but it will only be for a little while."

Emily crinkled her forehead. "But you said I could never stay by myself. Not even in the car."

"I know that, but tonight is different. I can't find anyone to come over and I have to work." Emily looked out the kitchen window toward Greta's house. "Look at me," Tracy said.

Emily looked down at the table and cast her eyes up at her mother.

"Can you do this? Can you stay in the house by yourself and go to bed when the clock looks like this?"

Emily was quiet, playing with the food on her plate. "What about a bath?"

"Not tonight," Tracy said. She knew that Emily finally understood what she was saying. "You can play in your room or watch the

Beauty and the Beast video that's in the VCR but don't answer the door if someone knocks. If someone knocks you turn the TV off and play a pretend game of not being here. Okay?"

Emily nodded.

"I'm going to call as often as I can but if anyone else calls just say I'm in the bathtub and will have to call them back."

"But you won't be in the bathtub. You'll be at work."

"I know that but I don't want anyone else to know that. I don't want them to know that you're here by yourself." She lit a cigarette and puffed till the end crinkled and glowed red. "So what time are you going to bed?"

Emily pointed to the clock.

"Right. Are you answering the door?"

Emily shook her head.

"If someone calls for me what are you saying?"

"You're in the bathtub."

"Right." Tracy took another puff and shook her head. She was crazy for trying this. No one leaves a five-year-old alone but she didn't know what else to do. She was already behind in rent payment and her car needed two new tires. She grabbed her purse and knelt in front of Emily. "I'll tell you what. In a few days we'll make a trip down by the river and watch the fireworks and eat funnel cakes." Emily's eyes brightened. Tracy pushed the butt of the cigarette into an ashtray. "Okay, I'm locking the door behind me. Do not open it at all for any reason. Stay in the house and go to bed. Do you understand?"

Emily nodded and sucked milk through a heart-shaped straw.

Tracy pulled Emily in to her chest and kissed her forehead. "I love you so much."

"Love you, too," Emily said, clenching the straw between her teeth.

Tracy leaned down toward Emily. "Give me a kiss."

Emily spat out the straw and kissed her mother. Tracy kissed her over and over and moved toward the door. "Don't open this. Don't come near it. Don't even look at it. Keep it closed and locked and go to bed at eight-thirty. I love you." Emily waved and watched milk zip through the straw.

I had just gone upstairs to get ready for bed that July evening when the phone rang. Since it was eleven-fifteen I assumed the call must be work related. "Hello."

"Patricia, this is Dispatch." It was the dispatcher for the Department of Family Services. "We have a situation that needs attention. A child needs to be placed in protective services." I took down the rest of the information and directions and got dressed.

Two squad cars were in the driveway when I arrived at midnight. I showed an officer my card and entered the home. I could see Emily sitting on her bed trying to look through a book with an officer sitting beside her. "Was anyone with her?" I asked.

"She said someone was holding her hand but if someone was here they left before we got here. Maybe the sitter got tired of waiting and went home."

"Does she know?" I asked.

"We haven't told her specifics," an officer said. "We can bring in a chaplain from the unit."

I shook my head. "That's all right. She's waited long enough." I walked toward the bedroom and smiled at the little girl. She reached for the teddy bear next to her and the officer left the room. I sat down beside her on the bed. "Hi, Emily. My name's Patricia."

"Are you a friend of my mom's?"

"No. I'm a social worker and I help take care of kids and families."

"Are you going to help take care of me and my mom?" She hugged her teddy bear tight, waiting for what I was about to say.

My heart broke for her but I knew I

couldn't struggle for the words; I had to be honest. "Emily, your mom was in a terrible car accident tonight."

Her face had no expression.

"She got hurt really bad and died before the ambulance could get her to the hospital."

She stared at the floor.

"Do you understand?"

She nodded although I don't believe she did comprehend what was happening.

"Am I in trouble?"

"No, no. You're not in trouble at all. We're here because we want to make sure you're all right. Your mom told a policeman that you were here because she wanted to make sure you were safe."

She looked up at me, confused.

"A policeman was helping your mom and you were the first thing on her mind. She told him that you were here."

Emily buried her face in the bear and rocked side to side before reaching her arms for me. I lifted her up and held her on my lap. She put her arms around my neck and I could feel the soft fur of the teddy bear up against my face. An officer walked by the door, looking in. Emily didn't cry; she just simply held on to me and remained quiet. I rubbed her back and rocked her back and forth. The master's degree in counseling I received seven years earlier to further equip me as a social worker never seemed adequate to help me through a situation like this.

"Will my mom ever come home?" she finally asked. My heart sank.

I turned her so she could see me. "No, honey. She won't." She leaned her head on my shoulder and didn't speak. No matter how old you are, those words always take your breath, leaving you numb. I knew it was too much to take in.

"Can I stay here?"

"I'll need to take you to a house where you can be safe."

"But I'm safe in my room." She picked up a clock beside her bed. "When the clock looks like this I turn off the video and go to bed. I do everything like my mom says."

I knew then that there hadn't been a sitter but that Emily's mom had left her alone. The circumstances of why Emily was alone would come out later but I knew that she had been cared for and loved.

I held her hand. "I know you were such a big girl tonight and that you were very brave but I need to make sure that you get to a place where you can sleep and eat without worrying about what the clock says."

She picked up a stuffed bunny rabbit and held it in her arms. "Can I go to Miss Greta's?"

"The policeman said she's not home right now but I'll make sure Greta is contacted in the morning."

Emily was uncertain of what was happening. "Can I take my toys?"

I picked up the teddy bear and handed it to her. "Yes, and I'll pack some of your clothes. Okay?" I waited for an answer.

"Are you going with me?"

"I'm going to drive you there."

She shook her head. I hadn't answered her question. "Are you going with me?"

I patted her hand. "I won't be staying with you but I'm going to make sure that you have everything you need."

She was quiet as I packed up what few clothes she had in her closet and drawers. I noticed a small catalog sitting on top of her chest of drawers and it was turned to a page with a little girl wearing a flowing lavender-and-pink princess gown. In my mind I could see Emily turning the page there and setting it atop her chest of drawers so her mother could see it. If she saw it, Emily was certain her mother would get the hint and buy it for her birthday or maybe help her petition Santa for it for Christmas. I stuck the catalog in my bag. I held out my hand for Emily but she didn't want to take hold of it. She wanted to be held. An officer helped with Emily's suitcase and I picked her up.

She looked into her room. "Can I ever come back?" she asked. This was the end of her memories in this house with her mother. For whatever part I played in that I wanted to make sure that Emily had a chance to say good-bye.

"Yes," I said. "I'll bring you back." I opened the back door and set her on the passenger side of the car. She looked so small as I secured the seat belt around her. I thanked the officers, told them I'd be in touch, and drove her to the Delphys' home.

I woke up the next morning and opened the door to let Girl out. I looked through my notes and called the number for Tracy's mother. It was out of service. I tried the number for her father and it rang several times before he answered. He had been notified of Tracy's death by someone in the police department but because he had been in bed with vasculitis for several months he would be unable to travel for the funeral. I asked if he'd ever seen his grand-daughter, Emily, and he said after she was born he had, but then he lost touch. I got a current phone number for Tracy's mother and hung up. I dialed the number before I let the sadness of the situation sink in. Tracy's mother had also been notified of Tracy's death and was packing her bag for the funeral. I told her how sorry I was. "I have to take off work," she said, out of breath from running to the phone. "They don't like it when people take off work at the last minute." I was stunned. She hadn't mentioned Tracy or Emily.

"Emily is in a foster home," I said.

"They could fire me for this," she said. "I hope they don't but they could."

"Would you like to see Emily?" I asked.

She sighed into the phone. I could envision her throwing her arms in the air. "If there's time. There may not be any time. I've got to drive in and drive out. That's all the time they're going to give me off work."

"Do you know Emily's father?" I asked.

"If I knew who he was he wouldn't be walking around today getting other girls pregnant."

That's as close to a conversation about Tracy or Emily that we were going to have. I called Tracy's brother but he was single and worked the midnight shift at a warehouse. He was kind but made it clear that he was in no position to care for a child. I hung up the phone and doodled on the papers in front of me. This was the part of the job that I hated: discovering that family members can't or don't want to care for the children who are supposed to be close to them. It seemed the only person who cared for Emily or Tracy was Greta Larson. I called information for her number. An older man answered the phone. It was obvious he was hard of hearing and by the third time of asking for Greta I was losing my patience. He finally handed the phone to Greta.

"Thank you so much for calling," she said, her voice cracking. "I've been so worried and none of the neighbors knew what happened to her."

I assured her that Emily was with a loving family.

"Do you know anything about her mother's family?" I asked.

"Tracy's mom and dad are divorced," she said. "Her dad is sick and her mother is strange. I know she talked with her brother quite a bit, especially during the first year after Emily was born, but I never saw him. He lives a couple hours from here."

"Do you know anything about Emily's dad?"

"To be honest, I don't think Tracy knew anything about him. They were teenagers.

He probably went off to college, got a job, got married, and has kids of his own now. Nobody knows. And I'm sure he doesn't care. Tracy didn't list his name on Emily's birth certificate. I don't know why. Seems the least he could have done was pay child support, and the state would have made sure he did, too. But I guess Tracy thought that was a battle she didn't want to fight for the rest of her life. Poor thing."

Her voice trailed off and I could hear her clear her throat.

"She was too young to be raising a child. She never could make ends meet but she was a good soul and that little girl of hers is a sweet child." She was quiet. Greta was the closest thing to a mother Tracy had had for several years.

"Did you watch Emily at all last night?" I asked.

"No, it was our anniversary. Something in me told me that Tracy wouldn't be able to find anyone to sit with Emily but she kept telling me she could. I never should have left."

"So you don't think anybody was with her last night?"

"No, and I can't imagine how afraid that sweet little baby was when the police knocked on her door."

There was no point in asking Greta again about who else could have been with Emily because she didn't know. But the thought nagged me: who was holding Emily's hand? What if it had been someone from the neighborhood who knew Tracy wasn't home? What if someone had questionable motives for being alone in a house with a child? I pushed the thought out of my mind. I promised to stay in touch with Greta and hung up the phone.

Greta and Hal knew the landlord of Emily's duplex would want to rent it out as soon as possible and they didn't want anyone else to go through Tracy's and Emily's things so they loaded their car with empty boxes and drove down the street. Hal emptied the refrigerator as Greta packed personal items from Tracy's house into boxes: a few photo albums and home movies, some of Tracy's clothing she thought Emily might like to have someday, what little costume jewelry Tracy owned, and all of Emily's toys. As Greta packed boxes filled with sheets and towels from the hall closet a small package dropped to the floor. She picked it up, opened the box, and discovered a small silver cross covered with pink stones. She turned it over and saw there was an inscription: "For Emily — Love, Mom." Greta looked at the bottom and saw that it had been inscribed with the word "Christmas" and the year. "She was a good mother," Greta whispered. When the house was clean and organized and Greta felt certain that she had packed away everything that would one day be important to Emily, she stood with Hal in the doorway and took one last look inside the tiny kitchen and living room she'd been in so often over the past four years. She wiped her eyes and Hal pulled a handkerchief out of his pocket and blew his nose. They both wished they could have done more for Emily and Tracy but what they didn't realize is that taking the time to show love to someone is more than some people will ever choose to do.

Ten days later I was sitting at my desk in the office when Greta called. The landlord of Tracy's duplex needed the rest of her things to be removed so he could make repairs and rent it out. I had told Emily that I would take her back to say good-bye and now that time had come. I picked her up at the Delphys' and held her hand as we walked through the front door of the small rental. The walls were bare, boxes were scattered throughout the kitchen and living area. It smelled like cleaning agents and stale air.

"Where is everything?" Emily asked.

"Greta and Hal packed everything," I said. "They have several boxes of things for you. Why don't you look around and see if there's anything else that you'd like to have."

She held my hand as she walked toward her bedroom. The closet and chest of drawers were empty, the bed was stripped and the toys were gone. I looked at Emily's face and wondered if she really understood what was happening.

"Can I have my bed?"

"Yes," I said. "I'll have Hal come pick it up." We walked into Tracy's room and Emily sat on the edge of the bed. Her forehead crinkled but she didn't cry. I knew that she and her mother had probably spent many nights giggling or reading together in this bed.

She looked underneath the bed. "All my books are gone."

"Greta has them," I said. She opened a box sitting next to the dresser and began to rummage through Tracy's clothes. Near the bottom of the box she pulled out a pink sweatshirt with Mickey and Minnie Mouse on it. She took off her coat and put on the sweatshirt.

"Can I have this?"

"Of course," I said. "You can have anything. It's all yours." She pulled out another sweatshirt, a gray one with frayed cuffs, and held it. Tracy's favorite, I was sure. We found a box marked "Christmas" and Emily opened it. There were a few bulbs and tinsel and a tiny Nativity set. I watched as she walked through the boxes, dragging her fingers over the tops of them. We spent an hour filtering through boxes, sitting in the quiet, looking out the windows, and collecting things. When she was finished we walked toward the door. I turned to grab the handle and felt Emily's arms wrap around my leg. She didn't want to leave. She let out a high-pitched cry and fell to the floor and I knew then that she understood that she would never see this tiny duplex again. She'd never see her mother wearing her favorite gray sweatshirt and putting on makeup in front of the bathroom mirror. There were no more Disney videos while sitting on Mom's lap or snuggle time in Mom's big bed with her favorite books. She now had the impossible task of saying good-bye and she couldn't. I held her as she cried. We sat together in the front entrance and looked out over the boxes into the home that would now exist only as pieces in her mind. I wanted her to remember what it looked like and how it smelled and the love that had filled its tiny space. I prayed that she would never forget because it held her first memories. Nothing can prepare a five-year-old to say good-bye to her mother, but Emily did. I don't know how long we stayed; it doesn't matter. We left when she was ready. She held on to my hand and closed the door behind her.

I pulled on my gloves and got in the car, turning the heat on high. It was one of the coldest Decembers that I could remember in recent years. I tried to contact two foster families on my way to the Delphys' to pick up Emily but there wasn't an answer at one home and the other family had already left the state for the holidays. I pulled into the Delphys' drive and Karen greeted me at the door. "I'm so sorry, Karen," I said, closing the door behind me. "How's Eric?"

"He's upstairs talking to his mom. They've been expecting this and trying to prepare for it but . . ."

"You're never ready," I said.

"No." She shuffled her feet and I knew something was terribly wrong.

"What is it, Karen?"

"Eric and I are going to have to stay with

his mother for a while to settle the estate. He's not the oldest child but he is the only one capable of taking care of his mother right now. We need to help her move out of the house she's been in for forty-five years and get her settled into a nearby retirement village and we have no idea how long all of that is going to take. It could be several weeks."

I understood what she was saying. There was no place for Emily right now.

"I just don't know how we could —"

"It's okay," I said. "Don't worry about her."

"She's a sweet little girl," Karen said. "But the funeral and everything isn't going to be the right environment. I feel awful about this, Patricia. We want her to come back just as soon as we're home again."

"Thanks, Karen," I said. "I'll make sure she's taken care of in the meantime." Emily walked into the entryway holding her suitcase. Karen knelt down in front of her and zipped her coat. Emily looked at the floor. Karen kissed her forehead and opened the door for us.

"Tell Mr. Eric I'm sorry that he's so sad."

Karen smiled and kissed her again.

I helped Emily into the backseat of my car and got behind the wheel. I needed to find another long-term foster home for her soon. I drove through the streets toward Wesley House, a home built by Methodists during the Civil War to help care for widows and orphans. Over the years it had been used to house children six years and older who weren't in foster placement at the time. Emily could stay there for a few nights till I could find her a temporary foster home. I looked at her in the rearview mirror. She was holding her teddy bear and looking out the window. She hadn't changed much in the five months since I first met her. She was still quiet and her eyes held the same uncertainty I saw in July. I turned onto the road that led to Wesley House. I drove slowly and soon realized that I had let off the gas entirely and the car was coasting. Emily didn't notice. She continued to look out the window. I stopped at the yield sign before the entrance of Wesley House and sat there for the longest time watching her in the rearview mirror. She realized the car had stopped and looked at me. I turned to look at her and tried to smile but couldn't. She was afraid and I knew it. She held my gaze and my heart broke. There was too much sadness in the world. Five-year-old little girls shouldn't be faced with life without their mothers, especially at Christmas. My mother always reminded me that life was made up of choices. *Sometimes the choices you make will lead to trouble, and you'll have to deal with that,* she said more times than I could remember. *Other times, a choice may change your life, and you'll have to deal with that, too.* What I was about to do was against the code of conduct for social workers but I didn't care if I was reprimanded or even fired. I pulled into the end of the Wesley House drive, turned around, and drove away. I had no idea what that simple choice would mean.

I opened my garage door and pulled inside. "Here we are," I said.

Emily pushed the button on the seat belt and it released. I opened the car door for her and she stepped out into the garage. I opened the trunk and pulled out her suitcase.

"There's been a change of plans," I said, opening the door that led into the kitchen, "and you're going to stay at my house. Is that okay?"

She nodded. Girl greeted us with a round of wet kisses. Emily turned her face.

"That's enough, Girl. Lie down." She lay in front of Emily and wagged her tail. "That's Girl." Her tail was moving so fast that her entire body wiggled with excitement.

"That's a funny name," she said.

"It's not the most original but it did take us several seconds to come up with it." I could tell that Emily was apprehensive but she stretched out her hand for Girl. "Careful, she might lick you to death."

Emily reached toward Girl's head and Girl threw her head up to lick Emily's hand and Emily jumped.

"That's enough, Girl," I said, scolding her. She lay down at Emily's feet and whined. I looked at Emily, "Would you like something to eat?"

She shook her head.

"Something to drink? Want some milk or juice?"

She shook her head again. "My mom doesn't let me drink a lot at night because I wet the bed."

I had noticed in previous visits with Emily at the Delphys' house that she would often talk about her mother in the present tense.

"Let me hang up your coat, then, and I can show you where you'll sleep." I helped take off her coat and she followed me to the hall closet. I hung up my coat and turned to her. "Are you sure you're not hungry?"

She shook her head.

"Okay, let's head upstairs." Girl led the way and I walked into the spare bedroom. Emily stood in the doorway. I set her suitcase on the floor and sat on the bed. "It's okay, Emily. You can come in."

She came into the room and stood in front of me. I helped take off her clothes.

"Do you need to go to the bathroom?"

She shook her head.

"If you need to go during the night it's right there," I said, pointing into the hallway. "Are you ready to go to sleep?"

She nodded and I pulled the blankets down so she could crawl into bed. Girl jumped on top of the comforter.

"Girl, get down," I scolded. I didn't like dog hair on the bed.

"It's okay. She can sleep here," Emily said, putting her hand on the dog. Girl gave me a smug look and I knew I was defeated. I pulled the covers up around Emily's neck and over her teddy bear. She moved the blankets from the bear's face.

"He can't breathe like that," she said.

I smiled. "What's his name?" I said, tucking the blankets under the bear's chin.

"Ernie."

"Oh, Ernie's a good, solid name for a teddy bear. How long have you had him?"

"Ever since I was a little girl."

"Well, I can tell he's a faithful friend. Just like Girl."

She nodded.

"Would you like me to leave the hallway light on so you can see if you need to get up?"

She nodded.

I moved the hair off her forehead and squeezed her hand. I turned the bedroom light off and closed the door halfway. "I'm in the next room if you need me," I said, peeking around the door.

She lifted her head off the pillow. "Could you leave the door open big?"

I opened the door all the way and moved toward my room.

"Could you come sit here?"

I stood inside the door of her room.

She pointed to the chair beside the bed. "Could you sit right there till I fall asleep?"

I tucked the blankets around her again and sat down.

She patted the side of the bed. "Could you sit here instead?"

I sat on the edge of the bed and held her hand.

She closed her eyes and tried to sleep. "Could you lay down on the bed?" she asked with her eyes closed.

I paused for a moment; I was fully dressed.

I didn't even like to take a nap in my clothes because of the terrible creases it made.

She looked up at me; I was taking too long to make such a simple decision. There was nothing I could do. Emily was afraid. I took off my shoes and lay down next to her, resting my hand on her arm.

"I'll stay here all night if you want me to," I said. I looked at her and she nodded as a small tear fell down her cheek. I didn't say anything. There was nothing I could say that would bring Emily's mother back or provide any understanding of what had happened. I wiped the tear away and prayed that God would provide a home full of love for this beautiful little girl, and after her breathing grew heavy, I fell asleep.

Nathan Andrews stuck his head out of the attic opening. "Lights," he said, reading the side of the box. His wife, Meghan, stepped onto the ladder and climbed up to get closer to the box. "Don't climb up here," Nathan scolded.

"I can't reach it," Meghan said.

Nathan's body filled the attic entrance. "Then I'll climb down." He held the box on his shoulder as he stepped down the ladder toward Meghan then handed it to her. "Careful, it's heavy," he warned.

Meghan reached for the box and rolled her eyes. "This might weigh five pounds," she said, placing it on the garage floor. She put her hand on top of her swollen belly.

"What's the matter? Are you tired?" Nathan asked, climbing the ladder.

"I'm just standing here waiting for you," Meghan said.

"Is the baby all right?"

"Yes! It's just bored because we've been waiting so long for you to hand down what few Christmas boxes we have up there!"

"Don't call my boy an *it.* That's offensive."

Meghan smiled. "What if this baby isn't a boy?"

Nathan looked through the attic opening. "Didn't you say he jumped the other day when we were watching football?"

"Yes, but —"

"No buts about it. You're about to give birth to a card-carrying Steelers fan!"

Meghan shook her head.

"Garland and wreaths coming down," Nathan yelled. He threw the box and it landed at Meghan's feet. "Ribbon and tinsel." Another box landed on the garage floor. "Fragile," Nathan said of the next box, watching Meghan's reaction. "Nativity."

"Don't throw that one!" Meghan

screamed, stretching her arms up toward the box.

Nathan laughed and climbed down, closing the attic hatch. He bent down and started carrying boxes into the front yard. "Don't carry anything heavy," he said, looking at Meghan over his shoulder.

Meghan rolled her eyes and picked up a box marked "Lights." They had wanted to decorate the outside of the house sooner but Nathan's hours at the hospital kept them from it. His third year of residency in pediatric cardiology kept him busier than expected at times. Meghan didn't mind his schedule. She kept busy teaching and coaching high school track and when she could she worked on preparing the baby's room. She was due the first week in January and couldn't wait to be a mother. When she and Nathan married on Christmas Eve nearly three years earlier they'd said they wanted to wait five years before trying to have a baby but when Meghan started to feel nauseous during her first morning class she knew that their five-year plan was changing. They didn't know the gender of the baby and didn't want to know until the day of delivery. "Nothing is surprising anymore," Nathan told friends and family who would ask. "This is really the last great surprise that's left. Besides, I already know it's a boy."

Nathan began to string the lights around the small shrubs in front of their duplex as Meghan opened boxes, pulling out wreaths, handmade Victorian stars, and painted wooden angels. She pulled a wad of garland from a box and began to straighten it when a small box fell to the ground. She bent over and discovered it was an unwrapped gift. She turned it over to examine it. "What's this?" she asked, turning toward Nathan. He was on his back underneath an evergreen bush making sure each branch was covered from front to back with lights.

He peered between the branches. "Don't know. Maybe it's the key to the Harley you bought me for Christmas."

"Keep holding on to that pipe dream," Meghan said. She examined the gift and threw her hands in the air. "This is that same gift we found last Christmas. The one with no name on it."

When Meghan discovered the gift a year earlier, Nathan had held it between his hands. He was quiet and shook his head. "What's wrong?" Meghan had asked.

"Just amazed at how stupid I am," Nathan said, setting the gift aside.

"Why? What is that?"

"I don't know what it is. Four or five years ago when I was doing my emergency-room rotation a patient dropped this. I found it after my shift and said I'd find the owner and return it. You can see what good intentions have done." He had told Meghan he would take the gift to the hospital and see if there was any way to find the owner but he never did. He thought he had thrown the gift away last year but obviously he hadn't.

Meghan knelt down and held the gift in front of him. "Why do we still have this? I thought you were going to do something with it last year!"

"What am I supposed to do with it?"

"Just open it up and find out who it belongs to."

"Yeah. I'm sure there's a business card in there with a name and address on it," he said, stringing lights over a branch.

Meghan put her hand on her stomach. "I hope the baby didn't hear that."

"What?"

"Sarcasm at Christmas." She slid the gift into his coat pocket.

"What are you doing?"

"I don't want it here."

"Why not?"

"It makes me feel guilty and this should clearly be your guilt. The baby and I shouldn't have to suffer like this."

Nathan laughed and put the gift out of his mind. Again.

A bird flew into the window and I jumped awake. I rolled over in such a way so as not to wake Emily. It was just after eight. I hadn't slept that late in years. Girl followed me as I crept into my bedroom and took off the clothes I had worn to bed. I put them in the laundry basket and stepped into the shower. I had no idea what I would do today about Emily but figured that since the office was closed I'd have some time to call on my foster families. I put moisturizer on my face and tried to rub out the wrinkles around my eyes that made me look older than my forty-three years but it was no use. I dressed and more or less smeared makeup on and then tiptoed downstairs to the kitchen. I opened the back door and let Girl out and then looked in the cupboards. There was no cereal. I walked to the refrigerator, hoping I had eggs; if I didn't I wasn't sure what I'd feed Emily for breakfast. There were two little eggs in the bin and just enough orange juice for a full glass. Perfect. That'd be enough till I got to the store.

I heard scratches at the door and knew

Girl was ready to come back in. I opened the door and the branches of a spruce tree greeted me. "Are you going to ask me in?" a voice asked behind the tree.

"I never ask strange trees in," I said.

Roy poked his head out from behind the tree. "Get out of the way!" He pushed the tree through the door and dropped it onto the floor. Girl bounded into the house and jumped over the tree.

"What are you doing?" I asked.

Roy took his hat off and wiped his forehead with it. "Whew," he said, wiping the sweat from his neck. "Either I'm out of shape or I'm out of shape. It's one of the two."

I smiled and looked at him, waiting for an answer.

"I had to take Jamie Kramer back to Wesley House early this morning."

I nodded, listening. I knew he was aware of what I had done.

"I went into the office and they asked what happened to your case. The little girl you were supposed to drop off last night. I told them that one of your foster families called you on your way to Wesley House and you were able to take the child there instead. Said you must have forgotten to call and let them know."

I leaned against the wall. "You lied?"

"I figured I must have had a good reason." He raised his eyebrows. "Didn't I?"

"This is her first Christmas without her mother. I know it's against policy but for whatever reason I just couldn't take her there last night. Not this close to Christmas."

"I knew I had a good reason." Roy knew it was risky but he didn't say anything. A social worker had taken a child home years ago, long before I ever joined the department, and the child fell down the stairs of the basement and broke his leg. After that, it became departmental policy that social workers could not take a child home under any circumstances. There was just too great a risk that the child could get hurt. We all followed the policy but off the record we had, at some time or another, taken a child home for a meal or a bath or an overnight stay. Sometimes it's just the right thing to do.

I looked down at the tree. "What's this?"

Roy picked up the tree and dragged it into the living room. "This is a Christmas tree. People decorate them during this time of year and put gifts under them."

I smiled. Roy didn't want Emily to wake up in a house without Christmas spirit. Roy tried to be gruff and rough around the edges but everyone who worked with him knew otherwise. He had a big soul and a bigger heart.

"It was tradition in our house to always put the tree up on the day after Thanksgiving. My grandkids helped me put my tree up this year." He stopped and looked at the tree. "Every child should put up a Christmas tree."

"You're a good person, you know that, Roy Braeden?"

He waved his hand to hush me. "Come on, now, I need to get going. I'm supposed to watch my grandkids today. Do you have decorations?"

I thought for a moment and grimaced.

He shook his head and opened the front door, reaching for several boxes and bags on the porch. Roy had everything we'd need to decorate the tree.

"Did you buy all these?"

"Well, at some point I did. I've been married twice, you know!"

I laughed and helped drag in the rest of the boxes. "She might not want to," I said, rummaging through a bag.

"Yes, she will," he said. "Kids love Christmas, no matter how sad their circumstances might be." He placed the tree in a stand in the corner, making sure it was straight. "Why in the world do people have to deal with death during the Christmas . . . ?" He stopped and looked at me.

"Death doesn't take a holiday," I said, opening a box of bulbs.

Roy pulled a large reindeer out of a box and set it on the hearth. "His nose used to glow until my grandsons performed rhino-plasty surgery on him a few years ago. He's seen better days but kids still love him. After his surgery we named him Warren because it's a name as dull as his nose."

Roy pulled a miniature jewelry box out of a bag and handed it to me. "Could you wrap this and give it to her? She can open it now or wait for Christmas — whatever she wants to do. My grand-daughter loves her jewelry box like this. It's filled with all sorts of gaudy beads and rings and there's a little ballerina that spins around. Do you have wrapping paper?"

I shook my head and Roy sighed, burrowing through another bag. He handed me a roll. "There's plenty there for you and Mark to wrap up presents for each other as well. I hear married couples still do that."

I walked Roy to the door and stretched to kiss his cheek. "You're just like a jolly black Santa."

He snapped his head to look at me. "Jolly? Is that another fat joke?"

I laughed.

"And when have you ever seen a black Santa? They're always white with pitiful, scraggly beards. There's one down at the shopping mall this year. The sorriest-looking Santa you've ever seen."

"I'm sorry I brought it up," I said, letting Roy out.

I closed the door and started to pull decorations from the bags. When Sean was a boy his little hands would pull tinsel and lights out faster than Mark and I could manage. He couldn't contain the excitement of being that close to Christmas. At first light on Christmas morning he'd run down the stairs screaming for Mark and me to follow. It was all we could do to convince him to open only half his presents so his grandparents could watch him unwrap the other half. Each year we'd buy him a new pair of sneakers and he'd pull them on and jump to his feet. "Look how high I can jump," he said, reaching for the ceiling. "Look how fast I can run!" Then he'd take off through the living room and kitchen shrieking as he ran.

At nine thirty I still hadn't heard Emily. I managed to organize the decorations before hearing Emily in the bedroom at ten. Girl followed me upstairs and pushed the door open with her nose. I saw Emily going through her suitcase.

"Good morning," I said. "Did you sleep well?"

She sat on the bed and nodded. Girl jumped up next to her. In the brief moment when she opened her eyes that morning I knew Emily had hoped, maybe even prayed, that everything in the last five months had been a bad dream. Reality is always much harsher than we expect. She looked at the pictures on the dresser behind me. "Who's that?" she asked, pointing to a picture of Sean.

"That's my son, Sean."

She studied the picture. "Is that your husband, too?"

"Yes."

"You're married?"

"Yes."

She looked at the building in the picture. "What is that?"

"That's a dormitory. That's where Sean slept when he was at college." She leaned her head against me and looked at the pictures on the dresser. She was quiet for the longest time.

"Does my mom know that I'm here now

instead of at the Delphys'?" A child psychiatrist had been talking with Emily for the last few months, helping her through her grief and although I had a counseling background I felt ill-equipped to help her. "Can she see me from heaven?"

"I think when people get to heaven that they are just overwhelmed with things to do."

"You mean there's lots of toys?"

"Yes. There's everything that you can imagine and more. But even though there's lots to do I think God parts the clouds every now and then when something special is happening so people in heaven can see what their family is doing." I felt a catch in my throat and couldn't speak.

"Sometimes I have dreams and my mom's in them and we're playing." I put my hand on the back of her head. "Then I wake up and she's not here." We were both quiet. "She can never come back, can she?"

Karen Delphy had told me that Emily often asked if her mother could come back. I felt tears coming but lifted my head so they wouldn't fall. "No."

"Do you think she wants to come back?" I'd never thought about that question before. Once someone was in heaven would they want to come back to the life they had?

It took me off guard and I thought for a moment. "Do you think she wants to come back?" Emily asked again.

"No," I said, whispering. "I don't think heaven is a place that you'll ever want to leave. But I do think she'd like you there with her." I felt my heart beating faster. I needed to change the subject. "Are you hungry? You must be starving."

She nodded and I gave her a fresh washcloth and towel in the bathroom so she could wash her face. I went to her suitcase and pulled out a pair of cotton pants and a red sweater with Snoopy on it. I helped her dress and thought of all those mornings I'd helped Sean. Just when I'd get his clothes stripped off he'd run down the hall screaming, hoping I'd chase him. I brushed Emily's blond hair and pulled it into a ponytail. I looked at her. She had deep brown eyes and olive-colored skin. She was a beautiful little girl. "Come on," I said, offering her my hand. "Let's get something to eat."

We walked down the stairs and Emily saw the Christmas tree and decorations. Her eyes widened. "Did Santa come?"

"One of his helpers did," I said, thinking of Roy. "He said he brought all this for you."

She stood still and surveyed everything that was there. "Where's the angel?" she said, moving tinsel and bulbs out of the way. "Where is she?" I helped her look and we discovered her at the bottom of a bag full of garland. Emily pulled her out of the bag and held her up, looking at the angel dressed in flowing white with gold trim and long blond hair. A scowl came across her face. "That's not what she looks like," she whispered, setting the angel down. She was disappointed.

"We'll go out and get another angel," I said.

She looked at me and didn't say anything. It had been so long since we'd had a child in the house that I was uncomfortable and I was afraid that Emily sensed it. "How about we eat first and then we can decorate the tree?"

She followed me into the kitchen and I poured her a half glass of juice. I pulled out the two eggs and a skillet. I couldn't remember the last time I'd made scrambled eggs but with the exception of overcooking them a bit they turned out okay. I set a piece of toast on Emily's plate and watched as she ate. She reached for her juice and knocked it over. It spilled off the top of the island onto the floor and I jumped, reaching for a towel. I wiped up the floor and grabbed a handful of paper towels for the side of the island; it was splattered with wet marks. Emily looked stricken and I realized my reaction had been too much. After all, it was just a little juice. What was wrong with me?

I smiled at her. "It's okay," I said, throwing the paper towels away. "Not a big deal at all."

She didn't believe me.

"Would you like more juice?"

She nodded and I poured the rest of the juice into her glass.

"Where's your husband?" she asked, moving the food around on her plate. She didn't look at me. In fact, since I'd picked her up she'd looked me in the eyes only once.

"He should be driving home from work," I said. I realized I hadn't called Mark to tell him about Emily.

"Where does he work?"

"He flies airplanes."

"My friend Alex flies airplanes, too."

"Really? Well, Alex and Mark will have to get together!"

She nodded and took a bite of egg. She saw a picture of Sean on the kitchen counter. "Is he at college now?"

"No."

She took a bite of toast. It was so quiet in the house that I could hear her chew. "Does

he live here?"
"No."
She moved the food around on her plate before taking another bite. She still wasn't looking at me.
"Will he be here to decorate the Christmas tree?"
"No."
"Will he be here for Christmas?"
"No."
"He's not coming home?"
"No."
"Why not?"
"Because he's in heaven."

FOUR

> Hope is not the conviction that something will turn out well, but the certainty that something makes sense regardless of how it turns out.
>
> — Vaclav Havel

Sean was a sophomore in college when he died. He was going to drive home on December 23, the last day of classes, and would be here for three weeks but he changed his plans when he learned Mark's schedule had changed and he had to work on the 23rd and 24th for a pilot who was in the hospital. "Since Dad has to work I'd rather come home the next day," he said. "Dr. Tamblyn said that if I want to work helping set up the new equipment in the media lab that he'll pay me the same kind of money professionals get. He asked me and another guy in class because he thinks we're his best students."

I didn't want him to wait another day to come home but I could hear the excitement in his voice. "I wonder if maybe your professor could set everything up when you return after the New Year?"

"No, Mom. He needs all this set up before everybody gets back. We can have nearly everything installed on the twenty-third and twenty-fourth."

I sighed. I really wanted him to come home on the 23rd but one more day wouldn't make that big of a difference.

"What time will you be here on the twenty-fourth?"

"By nine o'clock at the latest." Mark's flight landed at ten so that meant I'd be alone on Christmas Eve. I hated it but I knew Sean really wanted to do this.

"Okay, just keep me up to date."

I used those two days to finish cleaning the house, get all the grocery shopping done, and start baking. Mom and Dad and Richard and his family were coming over for Christmas for the very first time. Usually we spent Christmas at my parents' or Mark's parents' house. I baked a German chocolate cake and chocolate pecan pie before realizing that neither Richard nor

Dad liked nuts. I made a batch of peanut butter fudge. Surely that was more than enough to satisfy every sweet tooth in the house. Just to be certain I started a batch of sugar cookies when Girl wanted out. I walked outside with her and was away from the phone for only a few minutes. When I filled Girl's water dish I saw the flashing light on the answering machine. It was Sean.

"Hey, Mom, I'm on the road," he said. "I left an hour ago so I'll see you in a couple more. I'm going to be losing cell service in a few minutes but call if you need me. See you in a little while. Love ya."

I dialed the cell number but it went right to voice mail. I knew he was driving through a pocket where his cell didn't work. I'd try again later. I finished the sugar cookies and put them in the fridge to cool before I rolled them out. I cleaned up my mess, which was particularly big, and looked at the clock. Sean would be home in less than an hour. I dried my hands so I could call him but the phone rang before I could do it.

"Mrs. Addison," the voice on the other end said.

"Yes." I couldn't imagine what sort of telemarketer was brazen enough to call on Christmas Eve.

"Your son, Sean, has been in an accident."

I felt the blood leave my head and my heart raced. Which hospital did she say she was with? Could she repeat that again? Where is it located? How is he? She didn't know anything. I hung up the phone. My head was spinning and the wind had been knocked out of me. Where was Mark? He was flying. I had to call the airline so they could get a message to him. I dialed a number but got it wrong. I dialed a different number but got it wrong again. In frustration I pulled out the phone book but couldn't remember the name of the airline! It was in my cell phone. I'd call from the road. I needed to call Mom and Dad first so they could go with me. I pushed speed dial on my cell phone but they weren't home and they didn't have a cell phone. I pulled the car onto the road and headed in the direction of the highway. Did I put the garage door down? Did I even lock the doors? I didn't care. I sped through the streets of our neighborhood and onto the highway.

"Please keep Sean safe," I prayed. "Oh, please, Lord, please help him. Please." I prayed over and over again, repeating the same things. I couldn't think straight to put anything together beyond "Please, please, please." I fumbled with my cell phone and called the airline but heard a fast busy signal in my ear. I dialed it again and heard the same fast signal. I screamed. There was either a problem with service on my end or with theirs. "Please let him be alive and safe," I prayed, pushing redial. There was that same fast busy signal again. I threw the phone down. I didn't know what to do. Did I just pass the exit? I picked up the scrap piece of paper on which I'd scribbled out the general directions. Exit 218. Was that 218 that I passed? She said it would take about forty-five minutes but I had no idea how long I'd been driving. Here was another exit . . . 217. One exit away. I ran stop signs and red lights and saw a large white building in the distance. I gunned the engine and pulled into the drive leading to the emergency room.

I ran through the parking lot and into the hospital. There was a group of people behind the desk but they seemed to be moving in slow motion. Were they floating or was I? I tried to walk to the desk. Something was wrong with my legs. It was hard to move. "I'm looking for my son." No one paid attention, or if they did, they didn't pay attention quickly enough. I ran down the hall toward a young man with a white jacket and a name tag. I looked at it briefly.

It was on the list of names Mark and I had chosen for Sean but I forgot the young man's name the moment I saw it. "I need to know where my son is," I said. "He's here. I need to know where he is." I was getting frantic. The young man walked me toward the desk where no one had paid attention to me.

"What's his name?" he asked.

"Sean Addison," I blurted out. "Someone called and said he's been in a car accident."

The young man stopped when he heard Sean's name. "I'll get the doctor," he said. When I saw that young man's face and heard the change in his voice I knew that something terrible had happened and it was as if ice water rushed through my veins. The sensation almost brought me to my knees. I was shaking and weak but ran after him.

"I want to see Sean," I said, catching up to him.

He nodded but wouldn't look at me. "I'll send the doctor out right now," he said, moving toward a door. He disappeared and I could hear my heart beating in my ears. I began looking in each room for Sean but I couldn't find him. When I saw the young man I ran toward him. "The doctor's in surgery right now but will be out when he's finished." I could tell by his demeanor that he was trying to avoid any further conversation with me. He tried to get away but I grabbed his arm.

"You tell me."

He looked at me.

"You tell me what has happened to my son."

"We really should wait for the doctor," he said.

"Tell me what happened to my son!" I screamed. I could tell by the look on his face that I was putting this young man in an awkward situation but I didn't flinch. I had to know.

"He fell asleep and drove under a semi that was parked on the side of the highway."

My heart leaped to my throat.

"The paramedics brought him here and he was conscious. He was able to talk to us."

I nodded.

"But we could see that there had been a lot of damage." He spoke slowly. "I'm so sorry, Mrs. Addison. Sean's injuries were too severe and he died on the operating table before we could help him."

There are no words for that moment. My heart hadn't stopped racing since I received the phone call but now it had been slammed into a brick wall. My vision blurred and I felt myself falling. The young man helped me to a chair. Where was Mark? Where were Mom and Dad? Why was I sitting here with this stranger when there were sugar cookies to roll out at home? Sean had called and said he'd be home in a little bit and I needed to get everything done. I heard laughter in front of me. Two nurses were sharing a story with someone at the desk and their laughs rang through my ears at deafening levels.

"Can I get you some water?"

Who said that? I stared at the young man next to me and shook my head. "What did he say?"

The young man looked at me.

"When you said Sean was able to speak to you. What did he say?"

He paused and pushed away an imaginary piece of lint off his pants.

"He told us his name and where he lived and he said that you were home alone tonight waiting for him."

I felt tears streaming down my face.

"Then he said that he wanted you and his dad to know that he always loved you. Always."

I put my face in my hands and wept and wanted death to snatch me as quickly as it had my son. I wanted to die sitting beside that stranger because I couldn't imagine leaving that hospital and walking back into our home ever again. Not a home without Sean in it.

"Is that all?" I said, looking at him.

"He wanted me to tell you to never stop loving the children. That's all."

I moaned and put my hand on my head, trying to hold it up.

"You should know that he wasn't afraid."

I looked at him.

"He wasn't afraid. He was calm as he spoke to me. Everything about him was peaceful."

"I need to see him," I said.

The young man nodded and led me through a door that I never imagined I would go through and when I did my knees buckled.

"If it would help, I can call a funeral home for you," the young man said, pulling a chair close for me. "They'll take Sean to a funeral home in your hometown."

I stood at Sean's side and nodded.

"Would you like to wait in a private room?"

"I'd like to stay with my son," I said.

"I'll make sure no one disturbs you." The young man left the room and I never saw him again. Days later I couldn't describe what he looked like to Mom because it all happened too fast. I was with that young doctor for a couple of minutes but because of the circumstances I couldn't remember anything about him except to say that he had been very kind.

After nineteen years of marriage, it was hard for me to separate my point of view from Mark's. Whenever I met people, I met them not only through my eyes but through Mark's as well. If I went to a new restaurant I didn't just sample the food through my own taste but also through Mark's. Marriage does that. We no longer factor in just our own likes and dislikes, observations, or perceptions in any situation without filtering those things through the eyes and heart of our spouse as well. But all that changed after Sean died. As hard as we tried, Mark and I could no longer connect. We were with each other but it was different now. We were bonded by grief but the trouble with grief is that no one goes through it the same way as someone else. Mark immersed himself with all things Sean. He watched our old videos of Sean learning how to walk, singing his ABCs, "reading" *Goodnight Moon* or *Chicken Little*, or dancing for Grandma and Grandpa. Mark would sit in Sean's room and read through his old school notebooks and look through our photo albums. He played Sean's last message on the answering machine over and over and every time he played it I left the room. I couldn't handle it. I couldn't hear his voice or look through photo albums or watch our old videotapes because each time I'd hear Sean's voice it was as if a new wound was opened and it made me feel raw inside. Mark's emotions were always front and center but mine were deeper; I couldn't pull all of my feelings to the surface and for the first time in our marriage Mark and I found ourselves unable to talk. It was as if my tears dried up and I couldn't cry anymore. I was numb. We tried counseling but I gave up on it after a while. I couldn't talk with Mark about Sean so how was talking to a stranger with Mark in the same room going to help? I wanted to talk to Mark but the words would never come and they wouldn't come because in my heart I blamed him for Sean's death. I believed that if he hadn't worked on the 24th I would still have my son. If he hadn't worked Sean would have come home as scheduled. Mark and I had been each other's closest friend and the love of our lives but after Sean died we were no longer available to each other.

I couldn't sleep at night. Neither could

Mark. I'd get out of bed and wander the house before going back to bed an hour later. Then Mark would get up and I'd hear the TV or the shuffling of books before he'd come back to bed after an hour or so. Two years after Sean died Mark got up in the middle of the night and slept in the guest bedroom; he'd been there ever since and it felt like the most natural thing in the world.

It was hard to get out of bed each morning. If it hadn't been for the children and families I worked with I'm sure I wouldn't have. Somehow Sean knew that. That's why he wanted that young man to tell me to never stop loving the children because the minute I stopped working with them would be the day I stayed in bed and never got up again.

I tried going to church after Sean died but after several Sundays I couldn't go anymore. "They don't need me there," I told my mom when she asked a year after Sean's funeral. "They don't need to see me sitting there with my long face."

"But you need them," Mom said. "You need people who care about you."

I didn't need them and I didn't want to be around them or anybody else, but I didn't say that to her. I just wanted to be left alone. I found that I couldn't even talk with Mom about Sean. It was selfish on my part; she had lost her grandson and wanted to connect with me but I kept her at arm's length. It was easier that way. Time and again she sat down and tried to talk with me.

"Patti, God promised that He would never leave us," she said after dinner one day.

I felt anger at what she was saying but didn't show it. "I know that, Mom."

"No, honey, you don't," she said.

I felt my jaw tighten.

"I just know that God was with Sean, helping him hold on until he could talk to that young doctor at the hospital." Her voice broke and tears flowed over her cheeks. I wanted to be angry but I couldn't. "If God left Sean during those last moments of his life then God's a liar, Patti, and I don't believe that."

I squeezed her hand. She could believe whatever she wanted to help her through Sean's death but as far as I was concerned God could have prevented the accident. He could have wakened Sean so he wouldn't have hit the semi or he could have saved Sean's life at the hospital. If God hadn't abandoned Sean I would still have him today.

■ ■ ■ ■

The kitchen door opened and I jumped. Emily was finishing her eggs and I realized I hadn't paid attention to her in the last few minutes. I looked up to see Mark coming through the door. "Well, hello," he said, looking at Emily. "I didn't know we had company."

"This is Emily," I said, trying to gather my thoughts.

Mark extended his hand. "Hello, Emily. It's very nice to meet you."

She looked at him and remained quiet. It was enough for her to get to know me — now she had to add yet another stranger to her life.

"My mom died," she said, as a way of introduction. I had wanted to prep Mark before he got home and tell him what was happening. I hadn't imagined Emily would tell him herself. I could see it took Mark off guard.

"I'm really sorry," he said.

"I'm sorry your son died." Her words left a lump in my throat.

"Did you stay here last night?" Mark asked.

She nodded.

"You can stay here as long as you like."

"Are all airplane flyers tall?" she asked, looking up at him.

Mark smiled. "No, some of them aren't, but we tall ones don't hang around with them."

"Are you going to help with the Christmas tree?" She was already at ease with Mark; he always had a way with kids. Mark looked at me and I tried to smile. "Santa's helper brought it."

"You mean an elf brought a tree?"

"Yes. My mom and me didn't have one last year but she said we'd have one this year. Can you help us?"

He looked at me. The last tree we had decorated was the year Sean died. That was nearly four years ago.

"I'd love to."

There. It was settled. The three of us would be decorating a Christmas tree and it'd be the first time for all of us in a long time.

"I meant to call and tell you about Emily," I said to Mark in the garage as he looked for extension cords.

"It's okay."

"She's sleeping in the guest bedroom."

He stopped. "That's okay. I'll sleep in the

other room." Sean's room. I turned to walk back into the house. "Where will she go from here?"

"I'm trying to contact one of the foster families today."

"But it's so close to Christmas. She's so little."

I knew what he was saying but Emily couldn't stay with us. We weren't foster parents. Plus, I'd already put my job on the line by bringing her home in the first place.

"Does she have a dad?"

"Somewhere. Who knows?"

"Any grandparents?"

"In name only."

"How did her mother die?" he asked.

"Car accident."

He shook his head. It hit close to home. He unwrapped the extension cords that were in a tangled ball and I walked back into the house. That was the longest exchange Mark and I had had for days.

I walked into the living room. It was a mess. Decorations and boxes were everywhere. In the months following Sean's death I began to clean and organize the house. It was the one thing I could control and I wanted things to be in their place and to be clean. I pushed the thought of the mess out of my mind. This tree was for Emily. I could clean later.

We strung the lights first. We started at the bottom of the tree and worked our way up. Then we hung a string of braided gold-and-green garland. "This is what a queen wears," Emily said, admiring a strand of garland.

"The king wears it, too, doesn't he?" Mark asked.

"No," Emily said, matter-of-fact. "The king wears purple and pointy shoes." Mark laughed.

I stood back to survey the tree. "I think I need to put more garland in this area," I said, pointing.

"Let me get it." Emily ran for the garland and rushed it over to me. I had to smile. Roy was right; despite what she'd been through, she enjoyed doing this.

The bulbs came next. I picked up a box filled with bright green, red, and blue bulbs and opened them. Mark picked up a red bulb and slipped a hook through the loop at the top. I bent down to open another box and discovered it was filled with angels. "Oh, these are pretty."

Emily ran to it and peered inside. "Let me see." She bent the box toward her. There were gold and iridescent angels piled on top of each other. "Angels," she said, clasping her hands together. "We have to make sure they're way out here on the limb," she said, pointing, "so they can see everything." As Emily and Mark decorated each limb I slipped into the kitchen to make some cocoa. I'd always made cocoa when Sean was a little boy and it seemed appropriate today. I stirred it on the stove and heard Christmas music filtering from the living room. Mark had pulled out some old favorites and I could hear him humming.

"Frosty's not real," Emily said, listening to the words of the song.

"He's not?" Mark asked. "How do you know?"

"Snowmen can't talk." She said it as if he really should have known that.

"Rudolph talks."

"That's because he's a reindeer."

"So Rudolph is real?"

"Yes! Don't you watch TV?"

I heard Mark laugh for the first time in weeks. I'd almost forgotten what it was like to talk with a five-year-old. I walked into the living room and handed a cup of cocoa to Emily and Mark.

When the tree was finished Mark took the angel out of her box. "I think we're getting another angel," I said, remembering Emily's disappointment.

"No," Emily said, pointing at the tree. "God put her in charge of all these other angels so she has to be on top so she can see what they're doing." She took the angel from Mark and looked up at him. "Can you lift me high?" He lifted her so she could place the angel and she fussed with it till she got her straight. "There," she said, indicating that her work was finished. I sat on the sofa to get a good look at the tree and Emily sat next to me. Mark straightened a strand of straying garland, then sat next to Emily. She was quiet and stared at the tree for the longest time. "Is that what Christmas trees look like in heaven?" she asked. Mark glanced over at me.

"I bet they're even more beautiful in heaven," I said.

"Can my mom see me right now?" She was remembering our conversation from earlier.

"I'm sure God has parted the clouds so she can see you."

"She sees the tree?"

"Yes."

"Does she see all the angels?"

"Yes, and she sees lots of angels in heaven."

"As pretty as these?"

"Even more beautiful."

"Do you think she's happy seeing me?"

I smiled and nodded. I wondered if Sean was happy seeing what his dad and I had become?

We had nothing in the house to eat so Mark offered to go to the grocery store. "Get some chicken," I said. "And maybe some ground chuck and hamburger buns. I'll need potatoes and bread, and oh, don't forget eggs. Get some more juice and milk, too."

When he returned Mark's arms were loaded with bags. He'd gotten much more than just the few items I'd mentioned. I pulled out boxes of cereal, bags of chips, blocks of cheese, a couple of boxes of crackers, soup, applesauce, several types of juices, packages of candy, and fruit galore. I put the groceries away and found a small bag filled with videos: *Rudolph the Red-Nosed Reindeer, Frosty the Snowman,* and *A Charlie Brown Christmas.* It looked as though Mark had our evening planned for us.

Emily helped me peel potatoes and put them into a pot. "Greta lets me cook, too," she said. I could have kicked myself. I meant to follow up with Greta better than I had done in the last few months. "I go to her house a lot and cook."

"You like Greta?"

"She's my favorite friend."

Now I really felt bad. I had to call Greta right away.

"Was Greta with you that last night in your house?"

"For a while, but it was her eightieth anniversary."

I smiled. That would make Greta a hundred and something. "So she was holding your hand?" For some reason, the statement Emily made to the police about someone holding her hand had always bothered me.

Girl ran into the kitchen and stole a potato out of Emily's hand, which brought an end to our conversation. I dried my hands and dialed Greta's number. Hal answered the phone and I asked for Greta three times before he understood what I was saying. "Go put your hearing aids in right now," I heard Greta say before she picked up the phone. She said they would love to come over for dinner, and within the hour they pulled into our driveway.

Emily ran outside and threw herself into Greta's arms. The old woman's voice cracked when she saw her. "You're okay," she said, holding Emily. "You're safe and sound and you're okay."

Emily nodded.

After we ate, Emily took Hal's hand and walked into the living room so she could look at the tree again. Mark followed holding the videotapes he had purchased. I caught a glimpse of Emily sitting on the sofa staring at the videos in her hands.

Greta helped clear the plates. "What's going to happen to her now?" she asked.

"She'll go into another foster home for a while and then when the Delphys get back she'll go back into their home."

"All that moving around," Greta said under her breath. "It's not good for a child." I didn't say anything. "Will someone adopt her?"

"I don't know."

"I've heard that older children have a hard time getting adopted. Is that true?"

I hated to say it. "Sometimes."

Greta dabbed her eyes with the sleeve of her blouse. I handed her a tissue. "When you said she'd go into another foster home, when did you mean that she'd go?"

"Soon. Probably tomorrow."

"But she'll be uprooted again and it's almost Christmas."

"I know, but the state requires her to be in a foster —"

"She should stay here till after Christmas,"

Greta said, cutting me off. "She likes you and your husband. I can tell. She needs to stay here." Greta said it as if her word was final.

"We're not set up by the state to be foster parents," I said, trying to explain. "I'm not even allowed to have her in my house."

"But it's Christmas! Doesn't the state understand that? If her mother was here and she was unable to care for Emily she'd be grateful that her daughter could stay in a home like this with people like you. How could the state move her right now after everything that's happened? How could you do that to her?"

I couldn't look at Greta. The state had rules that I had to follow but I knew she wouldn't understand that. But I knew, too, that she'd never understand that I just couldn't have another child in my house. It was too painful. A child hadn't stayed in our home since Sean died and I preferred to keep it that way.

"Come on, ladies," Mark said, calling from the living room and saving me from further conversation with Greta. He put *Rudolph the Red-Nosed Reindeer* into the VCR and sat on the sofa. Emily sat next to him. He put his arm around her and patted her shoulder. Greta sat next to Emily and Emily reached over and held her hand. I knew she was making herself feel safe. "Reindeers talk, don't they, Greta?" Emily asked.

"Everybody knows reindeer talk," Greta said, assuring her.

"Mark didn't know," Emily said.

I laughed out loud.

"Did you know they fly, Mark?" Greta asked.

"Of course! I pass them all the time in the air." Emily smiled the faintest of smiles and slid closer to Mark's side and I swear I saw him melt a little.

Five

You can't help everybody, but you can help a few. It's that few that God will hold us accountable for.

— Bob Pierce

Nathan Andrews was awake long before five-thirty, the time his alarm clock was set to ring. In the last six weeks Meghan snored whenever she slept on her back and he'd been awake for forty-five minutes hoping he'd fall back to sleep. He turned off the clock before it rang and stepped inside the shower. He wasn't supposed to work that day but Dr. Wanschu had phoned last evening and asked if Nathan would cover his patients today because he'd gotten a virus and was vomiting. Nathan dressed and leaned over to kiss Meghan before leaving. She snored more loudly and rolled onto her side, when the snoring stopped. "Great timing," Nathan said, closing the bedroom door.

Nathan drove to the hospital and took the elevator to the fourth floor, the pediatric cardiology unit. The nurses behind the desk smiled at him. "What are you doing here?" one of them asked.

"Dr. Wanschu thought he'd spend the day vomiting."

One of the nurses cringed and then they began to talk amongst themselves. "You know, something's going around. My daughter was vomiting three days ago and yesterday my husband started. I hope I don't get it."

"Dr. Lindall was sick yesterday, too," the second nurse said. "Better wash your hands a lot. Dr. Andrews, you better wash your hands more often today," she yelled toward Nathan. He smiled and agreed.

Nathan opened his office door and put his keys in his coat pocket. He felt something inside it and pulled out the gift Meghan had found and shook his head. He put it back into his pocket so it would be out of sight and out of mind before looking through the files of Dr. Wanschu's patients. He sat down and took a long drink of coffee but couldn't stop thinking about the gift. He sighed and pulled it out of his coat pocket, wishing

Meghan had never found it, because she was right: it was making him feel guilty. He picked up the phone and dialed long distance. "Hi, this is Nathan Andrews," he said. "Is Dr. Lee available?" He listened to Muzak for several minutes before he heard the phone click.

"Nathan?" It was Rory. Dr. Rory Lee was the attending physician in the emergency room when Nathan had done his rotation during his third year of med school.

"How are you, Doc?" Nathan said.

"I'm great. I'm a dad again!"

"Congratulations! Another girl?"

"A boy this time. Ben. What are you up to?"

"Well, I'm about to become a father myself."

His old friend asked all the right questions. *How is Meghan feeling? Do you know if it's a boy or a girl? Do you have any names? Yes, it does change your life, but for the better.*

"What's going on?" Rory asked. "Do you need help with something?"

"I have a strange question," Nathan said. "Is there any way to find out what a patient had as part of their personal items? A patient from four or five years ago?"

"A patient in the ER?"

"Yes. Does anybody keep records of what a patient brings in? Do they write the items down and include that in the patient's file or do they just bag the items and label it with the patient's name to make things simple at discharge?"

Rory sighed. "That's hit or miss. It's rare but there are those occasions when a nurse will actually write down the items but it just depends on the nurse and it depends on the day and how busy we are. What are you looking for?"

"I don't know, really. I have something and I'm wondering who it belonged to."

"You don't know who it belongs to?"

"No."

"You're just hoping you'll be able to wander through files and see the item written down as part of a patient's personal effects?"

"Yes."

Nathan could hear him sigh. "That'd be like finding a needle in a haystack. If you didn't know the patient's name then you'd be out of luck."

"That's what I thought," Nathan said.

"What is it you have anyway?"

Nathan looked at the gift in his hand. "I have no idea. It's still wrapped."

"Then unwrap it and give it to charity. At

least that way you won't feel guilty."

Nathan laughed. "That's exactly what I'm thinking." He thanked Dr. Lee for his help and put the gift back in his pocket. He'd unwrap it at another time.

The phone rang and I reached over Emily to answer it. "Hold on one second," I said, whispering. I put the phone on hold and was quiet as I moved to the side of the bed so I wouldn't wake Emily. I held the door open for Girl to come out of the room but she just lifted her head, looked at me, and curled up closer to Emily. I closed the door and went into my room to pick up the phone. "Hello. Sorry about that."

"Patricia, this is Sandra." Mia's foster mother. "I'm sorry to bother you so early but something's wrong with Mia."

"What is it?"

"I'm not sure but yesterday she would sleep for hours at a time and last night she fell asleep at five-thirty. She just woke up and I tried to give her a bottle but she's struggling to drink it. It's like she's out of breath or something and has no energy. I called the emergency pediatrician number and they said I'd need to take her to the emergency room at the hospital but I can't take her this morning because Jeremy is throwing up." Her four-year-old son had brought home some sort of flu bug from day care. I could tell by her voice that Sandra was concerned about Mia.

"Don't worry, Sandra. I'll take Mia to the hospital." It wasn't the first time I'd taken one of my cases to the doctor or hospital and I knew it wouldn't be the last.

"Thank you, Patricia. I really hate to bother you."

I washed my face and wondered what to do about Emily. I wouldn't be gone that long. *I can just leave her here with Mark,* I thought. I pulled on a pair of jeans and a sweater and was digging for a pair of shoes when I heard something behind me. It was Emily and Girl watching me. They looked so cute standing there together. Emily's hair was a mess and she was holding Ernie by one paw.

She looked confused. "Where are you going?" she asked.

"A little girl is sick and I need to take her to the hospital this morning."

"What's wrong with her?"

"I don't know." I pulled on my shoes and sat in front of Emily. She leaned into me and I gave her a big hug. She put her head on my shoulder. "Did you sleep well?"

She nodded.

"Can I go with you?" she asked.

"It's so early. I thought you'd probably like to stay here with Mark."

She threw her arms around my neck and held tight. "No," she said, frantic. "Take me with you."

I thought she was scared of being left.

"The little girl might be afraid and want me to hold her hand."

"I hadn't thought of that," I said. "You know, I bet she will want someone to hold her hand." It didn't seem like the best idea but I knew Emily needed to go with me so I helped her get ready.

"Well, where's everybody going?" Mark asked, standing in the doorway of Emily's room.

"We have to go help a little girl who's sick," Emily said, pulling a sweatshirt over her head. "Could you take care of Girl for me?"

"I can do that," he said. Emily followed Girl down the stairs and Mark walked into the bathroom so I wouldn't have to pass him in the doorway. We had gotten good at polite avoidance and sidestepping one another.

I drove through the town square and noticed that Norma Holt hadn't begun decorating the trio of fir trees yet. For the last couple of weeks I had kept my eye out for Norma but never saw her perched atop one of her ladders as she placed the enormous ornaments on each branch. I slowed down when I saw a city worker sweeping the sidewalk surrounding the square. "I haven't seen Norma this year," I said, stopping at the red light.

"She's got pneumonia," he said, resting his hands on top of the broom.

"Is she in the hospital?"

"Been there a couple of weeks. She went in with a broken hip and caught pneumonia."

"How is she?"

"Not good. She's seventy-seven and there ain't much of her." The light turned green and I waved to the man, saddened to think that I never knew Norma and that her trees would never be decorated again.

I pulled into Guy and Sandra's driveway and when I picked Mia up I could see why Sandra had been concerned. She was a sick little girl. Emily sat next to Mia's car seat and held on to her hand. "She likes me to hold her hand," she said.

I looked at them in the mirror and could see that Mia liked Emily. There wasn't a long wait in the emergency room and we were able to see a doctor soon after we arrived. He examined her but I could tell he was concerned.

"Do you have some time?" he asked. "Because I'd like to call Dr. Wanschu in pediatric cardiology to take a look at her."

"What is it?" I said.

"I hear a murmur and her heart rate is too fast right now. If she were crawling or trying to walk the heart would be more active but she's not involved with any activity right now. It shouldn't be this fast." He walked out of the room and I held Mia close to me. What could possibly be wrong?

"Can I hold her?" Emily asked, trying to wrangle Mia from my arms. I asked Emily to sit on a chair and handed Mia to her. She wrapped her arms around her as if she were carrying a load of firewood. We sat in the room for several minutes before the doctor came to see us.

"Hi, I'm Dr. Andrews," he said, extending his hand to me. He looked too young to be a doctor.

"We're waiting for Dr. Wanschu," I said, assuming he had the wrong room.

"He's unable to be here today," the doctor said, taking a seat in front of Emily and Mia. "He seems to have caught some sort of virus." First Sandra's son and now the doctor. "Well, what's wrong with your little sister?" Dr. Andrews asked Emily. I opened my mouth to explain the situation but Emily beat me to it.

"She's not my sister."

"She's not?" the doctor asked, surprised. "Well, I just assumed she was because she's just as pretty as you and looks a lot like your mommy."

I groaned inside but still couldn't get the words out fast enough. Mia was slipping from Emily's lap and I picked her up.

"She's not my mom," Emily said, looking around me. "My mom died." Dr. Andrews looked at her.

"I'm really sorry," he said. "My mom died when I was a little boy."

"Were you sad?" Emily asked.

"Yes. I was very sad."

"Did you cry?"

"I cried a lot."

She looked down at her shoes and thought for a moment. "Do you still cry?"

"Sometimes."

Emily stood and put her arms around Dr. Andrews's neck. She was comforting *him.* I knew then why Emily was supposed to go to the hospital with me. She sat back down in her seat and reached for Mia.

"I'm Patricia," I said, handing Mia to Emily. "I'm a social worker and —"

"I realize that now," Dr. Andrews said. "I'm sorry. It's here on the chart and I should have read through it when I came into the room."

"It's okay," I said, recalling Emily's hug around his neck. He put Mia on the examining table and she began to cry. I watched as he worked with her, making her laugh as he ran his stethoscope over her chest and back. He was a good doctor. Emily stood close to his side and watched every move he made. When he finished his exam Emily reached her arms for Mia and Dr. Andrews handed Mia to her.

"Do you know if she's ever seen a cardiologist?" he asked.

"I don't know but I doubt it." He was careful as he chose his words because Emily was in the room.

"How long has she been in the foster system?"

"We just took her to a home on Friday. The foster mother was concerned about her breathing this morning."

He nodded. "I don't think this is the first time Mia's exhibited these symptoms but I do think you got her to us in time." I wondered what would have happened to Mia if her mother had left her alone for another fifteen hours?

"What's wrong with her?"

"She has a condition that's called incessant atrial tachycardia."

"The other doctor said she had a murmur."

"A murmur is part of it. People can live their whole lives with a murmur. But when I put my hand on Mia's chest I can feel the force of the heart striking the chest and when I listen I can hear an additional sound when the heart beats. A gallop."

"What is that?"

"It's an abnormal beat caused by an enlarged heart. That's why she's been sleeping so much but still seems tired and out of breath."

I put my hand on Mia's head. She was poking Emily and laughing. Mia had no idea she was so sick.

"What does all that mean?"

Dr. Andrews leaned against the examining table and crossed his arms. "We need to set her up in a step-down unit of the ICU for an electrophysiology study. That's a test where we'll put catheters into the heart that will deliver electrical impulses so we can map where the abnormal heartbeat is coming from. Once we determine where the abnormal beat is we'll use one of the catheters to deliver a short controlled 'burn' to the heart tissue to eliminate the source of the irregular heartbeat." I looked down at Mia in Emily's arms. She was so tiny. How could her heart take all of that?

"Is it surgery?"

"It's not considered surgery but it's equally dramatic. If she didn't have this procedure her heart would continue to deteriorate." He stopped, looking at Emily.

"Until failure?" I asked, choosing my words. He nodded. "When would that happen?"

He looked at Mia. "It could happen soon. With this procedure her heart function should recover and the valve leakage should resolve but it's important that we admit her right away."

I never expected this. I assumed it was the virus that was going around and he'd send us home with some medications. I nodded. For the first time in my career I was admitting a child into the hospital. I gathered my things to leave the exam room.

Dr. Andrews knelt in front of Emily and Mia. "Mia wasn't afraid one bit and that's because you were holding her," he said to Emily.

She smiled and he stood to leave. "How long did you miss your mom?" Her eyes were anxious; she needed to know.

Dr. Andrews knelt in front of her again. "I still miss her."

Emily's face was blank. She was hoping he'd say something different.

"But not in the same way I did after she died. It comes and goes in waves. When I was in track meets or when I graduated from high school I missed her a lot. I just really wanted her to be there. When I got married I missed her because I wanted to look out and see her sitting next to my dad. It's not all the time but there are times when I still do miss her an awful lot, but that's okay." He patted her hand. "If I didn't miss her I'd be afraid that I'd forget her, and I never want to do that. So I'll go ahead and be sad every once in a while, because if I'm sad I know I'm remembering her and how much she loved me." My eyes pooled over and I pretended to need something in my purse. I don't know if Emily understood what he was saying but realized she'd understand someday. Dr. Andrews led us to a desk for admittance and excused himself.

I called Sandra and explained the situation to her. She'd come to the hospital just as soon as her husband could leave work to watch their son. She said she'd arrive no later than nine: another hour and a half. I filled out the paperwork needed to admit

Mia, filling in the state as legal guardian. For the first time I was grateful that Bridget had been arrested for selling drugs and was thankful she'd left Mia alone for so long. If she hadn't, I wasn't sure that Mia would have ever received medical attention. I took Mia from Emily and smiled at her. "Hello, sweet girl."

She smiled and kicked her legs.

"You're going to stay here for a few days. Now, you might be afraid every now and then because doctors are going to be poking around, but they're only doing it so you'll feel better, so don't be scared, okay?"

She giggled and I heard her breathing become labored.

I kissed her head. "You're going to be okay, Mia." *Oh, God, please hear me. She's so tiny and her life hasn't been good yet. Help her through this. Please give her a family who will love her. Please give her a strong heart.*

Emily leaned over and kissed Mia's face and head. She whispered something into Mia's ear and looked up at me and smiled.

"What did you say?" I asked.

"I can't tell you," she said. "If I told you it wouldn't come true."

I smiled. She had watched a lot of fairy tales in her five years. A man dressed in scrubs came and took Mia from me. Emily held on to my hand and waved as he disappeared with Mia around a corner. I had a sick feeling, as if he'd just taken my own child. Emily and I waited the last few minutes for Sandra to arrive.

"They're going to perform the procedure in a few hours," I said. I knew I needed to find a foster home for Emily so I doubted I would be able to return to the hospital. "There are things I have to take care of, so I don't think I'll be back today."

"Yes, we will," Emily said. "We have to come back."

I didn't say anything. I took hold of her hand and walked toward the elevator.

"We need to come back," Emily said, looking up at me. I pushed the button for the elevator. "Mia needed me to hold her hand because she was scared. She'll be scared again today and wonder where I am. When I was scared in my room she held on tight, tight, tight, and then I wasn't scared anymore. So I held on tight to Mia's hand, too."

I nodded but didn't understand. I'd forgotten how children ramble, throwing lots of thoughts together as they talk.

She looked up at me. "Can we please come back?"

What could I say? It was against my better judgment but Emily needed to do this. I'd just have to find a foster home for her tomorrow.

When we got home I sliced an apple and put it on a plate in front of Emily before making several slices of toast with jelly. Mark walked into the kitchen wearing a pair of jeans and a black turtleneck. He was so handsome. He bent down and hugged Emily. At our core, Mark and I were still decent people and we wouldn't allow the distance that was between us to hurt her in any way. Emily had eaten half of the apple when Mark saw Girl sitting by the back door. "All right, little miss," he said, grabbing his coat. "Let's go for a walk." Girl began to prance in front of the door.

Mark opened the door and Girl bolted past him toward the woods that ended our property line. "Can I go with you?" Emily asked.

He zipped up her coat to her chin and pulled up the hood. It stood at a perfect point and she looked like a packed missile. Emily took hold of Mark's hand and they walked toward the woods, an all-too-familiar sight when Sean was a little boy. He and Mark would tramp out toward the woods to "hunt" bear or lions, build a secret tree house that only men could know about, or collect leaves for me. "Man stuff," Sean said time and again when I asked what he and his dad talked about. I watched Mark and wondered if he and Emily were talking about "girl stuff" this time around, or maybe about her mother.

"There's so much sadness on this journey," Pastor Burke had said at Sean's funeral. "Life is short. Thank God, heaven is forever." I watched as Mark and Emily walked toward the woods. Life is short but it feels so long for those of us who are left to live without someone we love.

"Did you live in a castle when you and Patricia got married?" Emily asked.

Mark shoved his hands into his coat pockets to warm them and shook his head. "Not unless a one-bedroom apartment is a castle. Is it?"

She shook her head to let him know it wasn't. "Did you have lots of money?"

"No."

"Then why'd she marry you?"

He laughed. "That's a good question."

She sat down on a log at the edge of the woods and put her chin in her hands. Mark sat down beside her. "I think Patricia's pretty."

"I think she is, too."

She looked up at Mark. "Will she always be sad?"

Mark looked at her. Somehow she'd seen right through me and he knew it. "A part of her will always be sad, but she has memories of Sean and those are good memories, too. We had him for eighteen years, so that's lots of memories."

"My mom was my mom for five years."

"You can have a lot of memories in five years."

"Sometimes we'd skate up and down the street." She thought for a moment. "But she wasn't very good. She fell down a lot." Girl sniffed around the log and followed the scent into the woods. The wind blew and Mark pushed her hair behind her ears. "Do they know each other?"

Mark didn't understand. "Who?"

"My mom and Sean."

"Yes, I think they do." He put his hand on the back of her head and pulled her toward him. They watched Girl sniff around a tree in the woods and jump as a squirrel darted past her up the tree. Girl stood on her back legs and put her front paws on the tree, barking.

"Where do I go after I leave here?"

Mark was quiet. He didn't know and he didn't want to answer. "Patricia will find a really good foster home for you."

"Can I stay here?"

Mark looked at her. Why would she want to stay in a home with two fractured people? "It's not up to me," he said. "The state has rules."

"I promise I'll be good."

She looked up at Mark but he couldn't look at her. He watched Girl through the trees. "You are a good girl," Mark said. "But the state has rules and —"

"I'll do the rules," she said, throwing her arms around his neck. "I'll do all the rules as long as I can stay here." He put his arms around her and she pressed her face against his. "Please let me stay."

Mark didn't say anything. He couldn't. "Let's get back before we freeze through and through," he said.

I had the kitchen clean and in order again when the back door opened. "We're froze through and through," Emily said, chattering her teeth.

I pulled off her coat, hat, and gloves and felt her hands. "Oh, my goodness, you are frozen."

"Through and through," she said.

I grabbed a blanket from the hall closet. "You better sit by the fire in the living room and get warm," I said. She sat on the sofa and I snuggled the blanket around her. Girl jumped onto the sofa and I swatted her off. "Get off, Girl. You smell like a dog. Go to the garage. Go!" Girl tucked her tail between her legs and headed toward the kitchen.

"Can she stay with me?" Emily asked. It was no use. Since Emily had arrived I was outnumbered. I snapped my fingers and Girl darted back to the living room.

"Stay on the floor," I said, holding her head down. I made Emily some hot chocolate and took it to her. Girl lifted her nose toward the cup. "Don't even think about it," I said. I kissed Emily on the head. "I'm going upstairs to throw in a load of laundry but I'll be right back." I walked upstairs and could see Mark through the crack in Sean's door. He'd be leaving for work soon. I gathered the dirty clothes out of the hamper in my bathroom and walked into Emily's room to clean the clothes she'd worn yesterday. When I walked out of the room I saw Mark in the laundry room straightening the arms of a sweater.

"It says 'lay flat to dry' but I like to lay on my side," he said.

I smiled. It was the first time he'd said anything funny to me in months.

"Will she be adopted?" His back was to me as he worked with the sweater.

"I hope so," I said.

"She wants to stay with us."

For some reason those words hurt. Why did Emily ask Mark and not me? I shook my head. Of course she asked him. I had brought her into our home but I had been guarded. And she sensed it. Kids always do. I went through all the proper actions but Mark was the one who made Emily feel at ease. I sighed. No matter what I did or how hard I tried I would never be comfortable with children in the house again. None of that would make sense to Mark, though. I needed to approach him with reality. He knew as well as I did that Emily couldn't stay with us because we weren't foster parents.

"She likes it here," he said. Despite what Mark and I had become to each other Emily felt safe with us. He didn't look at me but kept fussing with the sweater.

"She couldn't stay with us," I said. "It would never be allowed."

We were quiet. For too long now we'd let the silence rule in our house.

"You've bent the rules before, Patricia. She could at least stay with us through Christmas. A couple more days aren't going to make a difference. It just seems that she should spend Christmas with Hal and Greta and . . ." I waited for him to say it. "And with us."

"I've bent the rules for an overnight stay, Mark. Never for several days. I could lose my job."

He stopped his work and looked out the laundry room window. "Everybody needs a break, Patricia; especially a little five-year-old girl who doesn't have her mother at Christmas."

"I can't, Mark. You know that."

"You can't or you won't? There's a difference. There hasn't been a child in this house since Sean died. Over the years you'd bring one of your cases home for a meal or something but not anymore. Why is that, Patricia?" I could feel heat on the back of my neck. I just couldn't have a child in the house. Not now. Not ever. It hurt too much.

"Because it's just never worked out." I didn't even convince myself when I said it.

"Well, now it is working out, and that little girl needs a place to stay for Christmas. Years from now I don't want her to remember being in a home with strangers after her mom died. I want her to remember that she was with people who cared about her. That's all." Mark had always been a kind person;

it's one of the reasons I fell in love with him. I crossed my arms and leaned against the door, staring at the floor.

"Then she'll stay," I finally said. "But aren't you working on Christmas Day?"

His back was still to me. "No. I rearranged my schedule yesterday." He continued to straighten the sweater.

I wanted to say something, I wanted to touch Mark, I wanted to help him with that stupid sweater or do anything that would keep us talking but I didn't know what to do so I walked into the hallway, closed the laundry room door, and went downstairs.

Six

There is a crack in everything, that's how the light gets in.
— Leonard Cohen

Emily was asleep on the sofa. Girl lifted her head when I walked into the living room. "Shh," I said, motioning for her to lie back down. The phone rang and I ran for it. "Hello?"

"You never answered my question," Roy said.

"What question?"

"Do you want to come over here for Christmas dinner?"

I paused before I answered. "I can't."

"Why not?" It sounded like he was eating.

"Because Mark's going to be home." The chewing stopped.

"Well, that's good because we weren't going to have enough food anyway."

I laughed.

"Do you still have your little one?"

I told him I did and that we planned to keep her through Christmas. If Roy thought that was a bad idea he kept it to himself.

"I'm going to watch Jasmine tonight so my daughter and son-in-law can get some shopping done. Do you think your clan would be up for pizza?"

"I'll need to ask Emily but she's sleeping right now. It'd just be Emily and me tonight. Mark's working." If Emily was up for it, we agreed to meet after I took her to the hospital to visit Mia. I peeked in on Emily. She had to be exhausted. So much had happened in one day. *Find a home for her,* I prayed, watching her sleep. *Please find a home where parents will love her.* Mark was right. Everybody needed a break. I sat down in the den and picked up a magazine. I was asleep before I finished the first sentence.

An hour later I jumped awake. Emily and Girl were staring at me. "Girl was dreaming and she woke me up," Emily said. "She was growling and whining because she was chasing another dog."

"She was?"

"Yeah. She was chasing another dog because he was taking away her bone."

I smiled at her. Her hair was a mess and

her sweatshirt was bunched up over her belly button. Somewhere along the way her sweatpants had been lost and all that was left was her pink Winnie the Pooh panties.

I reached out and held her hand between both of mine. "Emily, would you like to stay with us through Christmas?"

"Can I?" Her voice sounded relieved.

"Yes."

"Can Greta and Hal come, too?"

"That would be great."

She lifted onto her toes and Girl nudged her with her nose. "Are we going to the hospital now?"

"Yes."

She pulled on my hand and I got up from the chair. The doorbell rang.

It was Mom. I walked to the back door and heard her before I saw her. She was wearing a red cardigan covered with tiny bells so she jingled when she walked. "I tried calling several times but there wasn't an answer," Mom said, leading Dad inside. She saw Emily and raised her hand to wave. "Hi, there. I'm Charlotte. Patricia's mom." She leaned down toward Emily. "What's your name?"

"Emily."

Mom threw her head back. "Oh, what a pretty name! You know, Emily was one of the names I had picked out for Patricia. Isn't that funny? And you know what? You're just as pretty as your name. Isn't she, Les?"

Dad moved in next to Mom and smiled. "Prettier," he said. "How old are you?"

Emily held up five fingers.

"Five! That's the best age of all." Mom and Dad knew enough about my work not to ask Emily any personal questions beyond that.

"We took Mia to the hospital because she's sick," Emily said.

"Oh?" Mom looked at me.

"One of my cases," I said.

"And we're going to see her now," she said, pulling on the pair of cotton sweatpants she had abandoned in the living room. She hoisted them over the sweatshirt and I smiled. She looked like a little old man.

"We won't keep you," Mom said. "I was just wondering if you've thought about going to see the living Nativity." I didn't do it but I wanted to roll my eyes. I thought I'd made it clear that Mark and I wouldn't go to that.

"I don't think we'll do that," I said.

"Can I go?" Emily asked.

I knew I'd been beaten. "Yes, you can go

with us," I said. I tried to usher Mom and Dad to the door.

"Do you want to see the tree?" Emily asked. Mom looked toward our backyard assuming the tree Emily spoke of was back there. Emily took her hand and led her to the living room. I could see by the look on Mom and Dad's face that they were surprised, to say the least.

Emily ran to plug in the lights. "Now my mom can see it."

Mom looked at me and understood why I had Emily. "What a beautiful tree," she said, clapping her hands together. "Did you decorate it all by yourself?"

"Nope. Patricia helped and Mark did the branches way up high."

Mom was even more surprised now that she knew Mark had helped us. She didn't know what to think.

"There will be all sorts of gifts under here for Christmas and me and Mark and Patricia and Greta and Hal will open them." She looked up at my mom. "You can come, too."

I nodded. There. It was settled. Christmas would be at our house this year. Mom contained her excitement but I knew she was about to burst because the bells on her sweater practically rang out a tune as she bounced toward the door. She and Dad left and I tried to imagine the conversation they were having in the car.

Nathan Andrews leaned down and whispered into the sleeping ear of his tiny patient. "You did great, Mia," he said, stroking her arm. "What a strong girl you are." The procedure was over and with the exception of a few cries before it began, everything went as planned. Once Dr. Andrews ran catheters to Mia's heart he performed an ablation, selecting one of the catheters to deliver a series of short impulses to the tissue of the heart to rid it of the irregular beat. "Thanks for your help," Dr. Andrews said to the staff assisting him. He ran his finger over Mia's cheek. "She thanks you, too."

We found Sandra in the waiting room. "Has anybody given you an update or anything?" I asked.

"A nurse came out an hour ago and said they finished. She said it went well and asked me to wait for the doctor." So that's what we did. We waited, three people who really didn't know Mia but would do anything for her. It was several minutes before Dr. Andrews appeared. He smiled and Sandra and I felt relief.

"She's doing great," he said. "Strong

heartbeat, great pulse. She's feisty."

"She's had to be," I said.

"Well, hello, Emily," he said, kneeling in front of her. "Mia will be very happy to see you."

Emily smiled and squeezed my hand. "Did you fix her heart?" she asked.

"I think so. In a little while she'll be just as big and strong and pretty as you."

Emily beamed. I think she was having her first crush.

"How long will she need to be here?" Sandra asked.

"A few days. We'll need to keep an eye on her."

"We'll watch her, too," Emily said.

"Well, I'll make sure that the staff knows to give you anything you need," Dr. Andrews said. "Lollipops, balloons, you name it."

A nurse at the desk called for Dr. Andrews. "It's your wife," she said.

"Excuse me," he said. "She's pregnant so I never know! I'll have one of the nurses show you where Mia is sleeping." We followed the nurse as Dr. Andrews took his call.

"Was that Patricia Addison?" a nurse asked when Dr. Andrews hung up the phone.

"Yes," he said.

"I haven't seen her since her son's funeral."

Dr. Andrews put a clipboard on top of the desk. "When did her son die?"

"Four or five years ago. He was driving home from college for Christmas and fell asleep at the wheel." A physician interrupted before Dr. Andrews could hear the rest of the story. He picked up his paperwork and walked toward his office. It had been a long day; he was ready to go home.

We walked into the room where Mia was sleeping. Her tiny body was dwarfed among a tangle of tubes and wires. Emily gasped when she saw her. "She's all right, Emily," I said. "All that stuff just makes it look worse than it is."

A nurse stood at the side of the bed and smiled. "You can come closer," she said to Emily.

Emily stepped toward the bed and looked at Mia. "Can I hold her hand?"

The nurse nodded. "Just be very gentle so you don't move her." It wasn't a comfortable reach, the bed was slightly taller than Emily, but she slid two fingers into Mia's palm and stood still, watching her breathe.

"How long will she sleep?" Sandra said.

"It wouldn't be unusual if she slept throughout the night," the nurse said. "This was a big day for her," she said, patting Mia's leg.

"We should go so Mia can rest," I said to Emily.

She nodded and looked at Mia's face as if she was searching for something. She held her gaze and then squeezed her fingers around Mia's hand.

"Okay, we can go now," she said.

"I'll come back first thing in the morning," Sandra said.

"We will, too," Emily said. We said goodbye in the parking lot and I helped Emily into the backseat. I buckled her in and moved her hair out of her face.

"You've had a busy day," I said. "Are you sure you want to go out for pizza tonight?"

She nodded.

I kissed her forehead and got behind the wheel of the car. I watched in the mirror as she looked out the window toward the sky. Was she straining to see her mother? Was she hoping she'd catch a glimpse of her through the clouds? I wondered what she was thinking but didn't ask. I had grown to hate all the questions I was asked after Sean's death.

■ ■ ■ ■

I saw Roy's car as I pulled into the parking lot of the restaurant. I parked beside it and laughed to myself. His car hadn't been clean since he'd become a grandfather. The backseat was littered with coloring books, Legos, toy soldiers, ground Cheerios, and a naked baby doll. I held Emily's hand and walked through the front door looking for Roy and Barbara. I spotted Roy trying to throw a small red ball into a configuration of rings twenty feet in front of him. The smallest and most difficult ring to throw into was worth fifty points. After four pitches he managed to win a measly forty points, not enough for a prize. Six-year-old Jasmine threw a ball and it fell through the hole of the second-biggest ring, earning her twenty points. She jumped and squealed and braids all over her head bounced up and down. Roy high-fived her and saw us watching at the door. He waved us over and stretched out his hand toward Emily.

"You must be Emily," he said. "I'm Roy and this is my granddaughter, Jasmine, and this is my friend, Barbara." He took out a handful of gold tokens from his pocket and handed them to Emily. "Would you like to throw the balls, too?"

She nodded.

He slid a coin into a slot and four balls rolled toward Emily. "You can keep these tokens and play whatever you want."

Emily threw a ball and missed the rings. She threw another one and missed again. Jasmine stepped in to give pointers and when Emily threw again she earned ten points. She turned to look at me and I cheered. Roy and Barbara and I sat at a nearby table.

"She's a doll," Barbara said, watching Emily. Barbara was a tall, striking woman with high cheekbones and gray streaked hair. She and Roy had been dating for so long that his grandkids called her Grandma and she loved it. "So Mark is home this year, Patti?" she asked.

I swirled a napkin on the table in front of me. "Yes. For the first time in years we'll be having Christmas at our house." I put my face in my hands and shook my head.

Barbara leaned over the table and patted my arm. "Everything will go fine. Trust me, nobody remembers flat dinner rolls or greasy gravy. They just remember being together."

I nodded. "Our problem is we're not so good at being together anymore."

"Emily doesn't know that," Barbara said.

Emily came to the table and I smiled. "Can I go play that game over there?" she said, pointing to a small basketball hoop. I told her she could and Jasmine grabbed her hand and pulled her toward the other side of the restaurant.

"She's a sweet girl," Barbara said. "Do you have a foster home for her yet?"

"After Christmas," I said. "Mark said that everybody needs a break once in a while."

"Mark's right," Roy said. It made me feel better knowing that Roy was on my side. "We'll have Greta over, the lady who watched her quite a bit, and try to let her have a normal Christmas." Jasmine yelled for Barbara and Barbara ducked as if being struck from behind.

"Lord, that child has a set of lungs on her," she said, getting up from the table. Jasmine yelled again and Barbara held onto her head as if it would blow away. "Yell one more time. I don't think Canada heard you," she said, walking toward the girls. The waitress came and Roy ordered a large and small pizza and a pitcher of Sprite.

"Diet Coke," I said, catching the waitress before she left. "I can already feel the holiday pounds."

Roy leaned on the table and looked at me.

"You look terrible, Patti."

I threw my arms in the air. "Please, don't hold anything back. Tell me how I really look."

Roy laughed and made room for the pitcher of Sprite. "Did she like the tree?"

"She loved it." I swirled the napkin in bigger circles in front of me.

Roy cleared his throat. "Are you happy that Mark will be home for Christmas?"

I looked up at him and wadded the napkin into a ball. "I don't know," I whispered.

Roy looked at me and nodded. "Did I ever tell you about Margaret's wind chimes?"

I shook my head.

"Well, I never knew that Margaret loved wind chimes but one year we went to visit my mother and on our way home we stopped at a restaurant that had a great big wraparound porch on it with all these wind chimes hanging from it. She kept me out on that porch for thirty minutes trying to find the perfect wind chimes for our back porch. She found a set that had bright colored birds on it and when we got home she wanted to hang them right away. So I hung them for her but I wasn't thinking and didn't realize that our breakfast nook windows are right by the back porch and every morning I'd hear those tinkling chimes, and they drove me crazy. Margaret loved the sound. She'd open the windows wide and just listen as they went pling, pling — pling, pling, but they drove me nuts. I couldn't read the paper with all that plinging. When she was out of the house one day I moved them to the front porch but when she got home and noticed what I'd done she moved them back. That went on for ages. I'd move them to the front and she'd move them to the back and open the windows so she could hear them. Back and forth they went until she got sick." His voice was quiet. "I didn't move them anymore after that. I left the windows open and let that sound filter through the house. When she couldn't get up anymore I put another set outside our bedroom window and when I'd lay down next to her at night I could hear them going pling, pling — pling, pling, and I'd fall to sleep. I could fall asleep to a noise that at one time drove me crazy." He took a drink of soda and cleared his throat. "I don't know why I told you that, Patti, except to say don't let this happen. If you and Mark get a divorce it'll be like another death in your family." He paused for a moment. "If I'm stepping over my boundaries you let me know, Patti, but I've known you for a long time and I knew Sean, too. And I know there's no way he'd ever want to see you and Mark split up or for you to check out the way you have. You've been part of the living dead long enough. I know what that society looks like because I was part of it for a long time after Margaret died. But at some point you have to make a decision to join life again."

I held my empty glass in my hands and rolled it back and forth. It was time that Roy knew the truth. "His bags are packed." I could sense Roy looking at me. "I don't know when he's leaving but he's ready. I know he won't leave till after Christmas. Not now that Emily is with us. We're both too polite to create any sort of scene with someone in the house." I paused. "We don't even cause scenes when it's just the two of us in the house."

"Stop him, Patti."

I wouldn't look at him. "I can't." I shifted in my chair, reaching for my purse. I wanted to end this conversation. "We just keep drifting and neither one of us knows how to . . . I don't know."

"Yes, you do," he said. "We always know what to do but sometimes that means an awful lot of work and opting out is easier. There's a divorced woman walking around this town with my last name who's a result of my taking the easy way out."

"That's not true, Roy," I said. "I ran into Ella the other day and she told me she dropped your name a long time ago." Roy rolled his eyes and I laughed out loud.

Emily fell asleep on the way home. It was only eight o'clock but the day had been so long for both of us. I helped her up the stairs and into her pajamas. She slipped into bed and Girl curled up by her feet. "Can you read to me?" she asked, rubbing her eyes. It was the first time she'd wanted me to read before she fell asleep.

"Aren't you too tired for a story?" She shook her head. I opened the top drawer of the dresser and found some of the special books I had been saving since Sean's childhood for my grandchildren. Neither Mark nor I had thrown them out after Sean's death. I picked up *Love You Forever.* I had read it so often to Sean that at one time I had it memorized. The pages were worn, some had food stains and were torn, but Emily didn't notice.

I read how a mother had a baby boy and rocked him in her arms. Then I got to the part where the mother sings about loving her son forever. I had made up a tune for the song years ago when Sean was a child.

Emily glanced up at me; she recognized the story. I read how the little boy turned nine years old and then into a teenager and then into a grown man with children of his own and after each stage of life I would sing again. At the end the mother is aged and she calls her son to tell him she is sick. Emily was quiet as she looked at the picture on the page. When the son came through the door the old woman tried to sing but she was unable to finish the song because she was too ill. I felt tears coming but kept reading. I choked on the words as the son picked the mother up and rocked her back and forth, singing the song she had always sung to him. I tried to sing but I couldn't. I couldn't even speak.

Emily sang out the tune I had been singing throughout the book. Tears trailed down my nose and I wiped my face. "It's okay, Patricia," she said, patting my shoulder. "The boy said he'd always love his mommy."

I nodded.

"It's not sad. It's happy."

I hugged her to me and cried over the loss of Sean and of losing her in a couple of days. It was the first time I'd cried in years.

"Thank you for helping me finish the book," I said, wiping my face.

"Maybe you shouldn't read it anymore,"

she said. I hugged her tight. She held on to my arm and I knew she wanted me to stay with her. I lay down and pulled the blankets up and laid them across her chest. I reached and turned off the light. She moved her hand around in the darkness looking for mine; she wanted to hold it. She pulled it onto her chest and took a deep breath. She was content. I needed to get up so I could let Girl out. I needed to check the messages on the answering machine, I needed to check my e-mail, but felt myself drifting. I was too tired to move.

At one o'clock in the morning Nathan Andrews awoke with a start. "It's her," he said, louder than he realized.

"What's wrong?" Meghan asked, lifting her head to see him in the moonlight.

"I just thought of something," he said, getting out of bed.

"What are you doing?" Meghan asked, leaning up on one arm.

"Nothing. Go back to sleep." He pulled on a pair of sweatpants and a sweatshirt and tiptoed toward the door.

Meghan turned on the light and shielded her face. "Where in the world are you going?"

"I need to open that gift."

"What gift?"
"The gift I found during my ER rotation."
"You need to open it *now?*"
"Yes."
"Where is it?"
"It's in my coat pocket."
Meghan sat on the edge of the bed. "Why are you getting it now?"
"I really need to see what's in that box."
Meghan put her feet on the floor and pushed herself off from the bed.
"What are you doing?" Nathan said.
"I'm going with you."
He tried to help her back into bed. "No. It's too late. Go back to sleep."
"Like I can sleep now! I want to see what's in the box, too."
"You're going to turn our son into a night owl."
"Trust me, this baby's already a night owl. It's been kicking me all night."
"A football player in the making," Nathan said, turning the light on in the hallway.
Meghan rolled her eyes. It was too early in the morning to argue. She followed Nathan to the front hallway, where he opened the closet door and pulled the gift out of his coat pocket. They walked into the living room and sat down.
"Are you ever going to tell me what you're

thinking?" Meghan asked.

"Do you remember how I told you that med students will never forget the first time they have to tell someone that a loved one has died?"

She nodded. "What's that got to do with the gift?"

"Four years ago, on Christmas Eve, paramedics brought in a young guy who had fallen asleep at the wheel. His car went right up under a tractor-trailer. I was part of the team that tried to save him. I saw this gift on the floor and I assumed it had to have been in his pocket so I picked it up and set it aside but there wasn't an opportunity to ask him about it. He wasn't making it and we knew it. We tried to save him but we couldn't, and before I knew it, there was his mother asking about him, wanting to see him, but he was gone. The attending physicians were busy and she was in the hall asking about her son. I was terrified. I couldn't look at her and tell her that her eighteen-year-old son was dead so I tried to find the attendings, but they had their hands full with two shooting victims so there I was trying to stay out of sight, but the mother was wandering the halls looking for somebody who could tell her something." He shook his head. "I hated that night."

"So this gift was with that boy who died?"

"I don't know. I remember seeing it the next day on the admittance desk and I put it in my locker so I'd be sure to track down who it belonged to. It didn't take long for it to get buried, pushed to the back of my locker, and I forgot all about it."

"How'd you remember the boy's name?"

"I don't remember. I can remember that night but I can't remember his name or his mother's face." When he went to med school Nathan had assumed that he would remember the faces of tragedy he dealt with but over time names and faces always blurred. He felt guilty until several doctors told him they found that to be their experience as well. Nathan thought of it as God's grace that he couldn't remember every detail like faces or names but could always recall the emotions he felt. "I think I ran into his mother this week," he said.

"Did you recognize her?"

Nathan tore the green wrapping from the gift. "No. But I only saw her for a few minutes that night in the ER and I was so nervous that I can't remember anything about her." He threw the wrapping paper on the floor, opened a black velvet box and pulled out an antique pocket watch that was nestled in the middle of a tarnished gold holder. Nathan took out the watch and hung it onto the hook at the top of the holder.

"It's beautiful," Meghan said. Nathan turned the watch over and read the engraving: *"Mom, Always . . . S."*

At the bottom of the box was a gift card. He looked to the bottom of it but again, the signature was simply *S.* Nathan picked up the phone and dialed.

"Who are you calling?" Meghan said.

"The ER at County. I'm hoping an old friend will be on duty tonight. If not, somebody else could help." He asked for Dr. Lee and smiled when he was put on hold. "He's there," he said, moving the phone from his mouth. The phone clicked on the other end.

"Twice in one week," Rory said. "What's going on?"

"Do you feel like hunting down that needle in the haystack we talked about?"

"Did you think of a name?"

"The last name's Addison. Check files for Christmas Eve four years ago. If you can tell me a first name that'd be great, but better than that, I'm hoping his personal effects were logged in that night."

"When do you need it?"

"As soon as your Christmas spirit allows

you to move on it." Nathan heard shouting in the background. It was another busy night in the ER.

"I'll do what I can," Rory said, hanging up the phone. It was a long shot but fortunately, both Meghan and Nathan believed in them.

Seven

> These are the hardest times, especially when those who are younger than you take their leave, and there are times when I forget and permit myself to think that I am in the midst of death. But this is not so. It is life that surrounds me. Life. Life that is meant to be lived, its riches to be extracted. No, the Lord's promise is not for those who give up, but for those who forge ahead . . .
>
> — Leonora Wood

I heard something in the kitchen at 6:30. I tried to move but my neck was stiff. Girl jumped to the floor and wagged her tail, pacing back and forth between the bed and the door. I managed to sit up and rolled my neck around. Emily was still sound asleep. I looked down at myself. I'd never slept in my clothes so much in my life! I was a mess.

I opened the door and Girl bolted down the stairs. Mark was in the kitchen lining the island with shopping bags. He looked at me and his face said it all. He didn't know if I was coming or going. "Is she sleeping?" he asked, whispering.

I told him she was. He pulled something out of a department store bag and held it up. "Do you think she'll like this? She kept talking about queens and kings and I just thought she might. I don't know." It was a princess dress like the one in the catalog. It even came with a tiara and a pair of pink sequined plastic shoes. I couldn't believe he'd bought it. He hadn't seen the picture.

"She'll go crazy over it," I said. He started rummaging through other bags and pulled out a baby doll with two different sets of clothes and a stroller, an Easy Bake oven, a puzzle, and Magic Markers and paints. His face was beaming.

"What do you think?"

I was amazed. "When did you do all this?"

"On my way in to work last night. Will she like it?"

I couldn't find the right words. "What little girl wouldn't?" He scooped all the gifts into his arms and began to rummage through our hall closet. I knew what he was looking for. I picked up the roll of wrapping paper Roy had left for me and handed it to him. "Roy left this for us."

Mark took his project into the den and closed the door. "Don't let her come in here," he said, opening the door a crack. Mark was excited about Christmas. I felt a rush of energy jolt through me. It was Christmas Eve! I had to get busy. I headed for the stairs when the phone rang.

"Hello, Mom," I said, knowing it was her.

"I bought a turkey days ago," she said. "What else can we do to help?"

"How long have you been waiting to call?"

"All night long, thank you for asking. Now are you going to tell me anything or am I going to have to play twenty questions?"

I laughed. "Emily's still sleeping and I haven't showered in two days. How do you and Dad feel about coming over here and helping me get some things prepared?"

"What are you making?"

"I have no idea."

I could hear her mumbling something to Dad. "I've got ingredients for fudge, pecan pie, and enough stuff to make a small batch of English toffee. I've also got sweet potatoes, broccoli, veggies for a green salad, corn, yeast for rolls, and potatoes. How's that sound?"

"So basically you have everything for a

Christmas meal?"

"Basically." We hung up and I ran for my Palm Pilot. I had to call Greta and Hal and invite them for Christmas before it was too late. The phone rang and rang and I groaned. Maybe they'd gone out of town to see their kids. A crackly-voiced Hal answered.

"I'm sorry to bother you this early," I said. "But we really want you to come over tomorrow for Christmas."

"Hold on," he yelled into the receiver.

"Why'd you answer the phone in the first place?" Greta said, taking it from him. "Sorry, he can't hear anything without his hearing aids. Who's calling?"

"It's Patti," I said, catching myself because I was still yelling into the phone. "We really want you to come over for Christmas to watch Emily open her gifts and to eat with us. Can you do it?"

"Oh, we'd love it. Thank you so much. I have some things for her and I found something that Tracy bought for her." We talked over our plans and Greta asked again and again if she could bring anything but I declined. I just wanted them to enjoy the day with Emily. I hung up the phone and ran up the stairs for a shower. I jumped in and lathered my hair. I felt a small sensation fluttering in my heart. I couldn't put my finger on what it was exactly but it felt like excitement. Despite the sadness and pain I wanted Emily to love Christmas so she would never dread it the way I did. I wanted to make this Christmas as special as I could for her . . . and for Mark and me. I turned the water off and stepped out of the shower when I realized I hadn't sprayed down the walls or run the squeegee over the glass doors. *Tomorrow,* I thought, reaching for my towel. I dried my hair and put makeup on, taking extra time to do it well. I convinced myself that I didn't want Emily's memories to be those of spending Christmas with a hag, but deep down I knew I wanted to look pretty. For the first time in years I wanted to look as if I were alive.

I ran down the stairs and saw Girl staring at the back door. "Did we forget you?" I said, rubbing her head. I opened the door and Girl ran toward the woods. I looked around the kitchen but didn't know where to start.

"What can I do?"

I spun to see Mark standing in the doorway.

"The gifts are wrapped and hidden so I'm ready to help." It felt just like the times when Sean was a little boy and we'd run around the house like crazy people getting last-minute things done.

"We need to put the leaves in the table." We hadn't made the table bigger in four years. I couldn't even remember where the leaves were. "And I'd love to hang some garland in the dining room — maybe put some decorations on the mantle and find our red tablecloth and that great big centerpiece with the pinecones." I was talking so fast I could barely keep up with what I was saying.

Mark held up his hand. "Let me go to the garage attic and look for all that stuff before you tell me anything else." He disappeared into the garage and I started to pull out the china we'd received on our wedding day. We rarely used it; there wasn't a scratch on it. *What a shame,* I thought. It was so beautiful and I kept it put away. I pulled out several pieces and began to wash them. I heard rustling at the door and looked up to see Mom and Dad fumbling with grocery bags. I ran to open the door and saw that the ground was covered with fresh snow. *A white Christmas for Emily,* I thought.

"Ho, ho, ho," Mom said, coming through the door. She sat the bags down on the kitchen table and looked at the stack of dishes.

"There's more in the cabinet," I said. "Once we get these washed and out of the way we can start baking."

"Is Emily asleep?" Dad asked. I nodded. He bent down and pulled out a set of books with beautiful illustrated covers. "We got her these." He read off the titles: *Alice in Wonderland, Anne of Green Gables, Little House on the Prairie, The Complete Tales of Winnie the Pooh, Curious George,* and *The Chronicles of Narnia.* I wondered how much they had spent on such beautiful books but I knew it didn't matter to them. At one time my mother had been in need and people gave her gifts she never imagined.

"Is Mark home?" Dad asked. I pointed toward the garage and pictured Dad climbing up our rickety attic ladder to find Mark. Mom and I worked side by side washing the dishes and drying them.

"How did her mother die?" she asked.

"Car accident."

She was quiet as she dried a large serving platter and set it on the counter. "Did you go to the funeral?"

"Yes."

"Oh, God, help her," she said to herself. Throughout our lives, if Mom heard of someone who had died or was sick with cancer or heart disease she would grow quiet and I always knew she was praying. She never said she was; she didn't bow her head or close her eyes or get down on her knees and fold her hands; I just knew. If Walter Cronkite showed a family involved in a tragedy or someone who had lost their life in a foreign country on the evening news she would say, "Oh, God, help them." When I was a child I wondered how many prayers had been muttered all over the country during those thirty-minute news broadcasts. "It was the prayers of strangers that helped us," she said to Richard and me time and again after our father left.

With the last of the dishes washed and dried Mom got busy making a piecrust for the pecan pie and I grabbed a pot to make fudge. I reached for my recipe box; it had been so long that I'd forgotten how to do it. A huge thud sounded in the garage and I was certain Dad had fallen from the ladder and was lying on his back on the floor. "Don't panic," he said, yelling in through the door. "Just a box of garland." Moments later he and Mark carried several boxes into the dining room. I never imagined I would see Mark and my dad pulling decorations from a box and discussing color scheme and placement. "That doesn't look right next to that red glass globe," Dad said. "Put that ivy-looking thing there." I could hear Mark move things around. "Yeah, that looks better. Now move those candles to the back. No, take them off completely. They don't look Christmassy. What's this?"

"That's a thing to hold Christmas cards," Mark said. I heard a thud as Dad threw the "thing to hold Christmas cards" back in the box.

"Here we go. Put that up there on the mantle. What is that? A candelabra?"

"Yeah."

"Put that in the middle and let's stick some candles in there. You got any candles? Hey, Patti, you got any candles?"

"No, Dad, I don't think so."

He walked into the kitchen and picked up the pad of paper next to the phone. "We'll need to write that down. If we go with that thing on the mantle then we're going to need green candles. No, red." He jotted something down on the paper and went back into the dining room.

"This garland is a crumpled, flat mess," Mark said.

I saw Dad scribbling on the pad again. "Let's get the real kind, the kind that smells," he said. "And let's get enough to wrap it around the banister going upstairs. Emily will like that."

"Write down some sort of centerpiece, too," Mark said. "This pinecone thing has seen better days. And put down one of those long things that run right down the center of the table." Mom and I listened as they dug through more boxes and pulled out what they could, commenting on usability, age of the product in hand, where it was purchased, and how they used to have one of those when they were a kid.

"All right, we've got to go to the store," Dad said. "Do you girls need anything?"

We shook our heads.

"I'm getting eggnog," he said, jotting on the list again. "I don't care if it's bad for you, I'm getting it anyway."

Mom didn't argue. She'd go back to watching his cholesterol after Christmas. I could feel that small level of excitement building again. It was going to be a good Christmas this year. I thought I heard something upstairs.

"Patricia!" It was Emily. She was screaming. I ran past Mom and bolted up the stairs into the guest bedroom. Emily was lying still, the covers pulled up under her chin. I sat on the bed next to her.

"Are you okay?" I asked.

She nodded and held my hand. "Were you afraid when you woke up?"

She nodded. I helped her sit up and hugged her to me.

"It's okay." She wrapped her arms around me and I couldn't remember the last time I'd felt so needed. "Do you know what today is?"

She shook her head.

"It's Christmas Eve. So do you know what tomorrow is?"

"Christmas," she whispered.

"That's right. And we're downstairs right now making all sorts of pies and candy, and I've invited Greta and Hal to come spend the day with us tomorrow."

She nodded but was quiet. "Do they have Christmas in heaven?"

"Every day is Christmas in heaven," I said.

"I want my mom to be here for Christmas." I pulled her close and rested my chin on top of her head.

"I know," I said. I kissed her forehead and squeezed her hand. For the rest of her life she would miss her mother, but the holidays would always be especially heartbreaking.

She looked around the room. "Where's Girl?" That was all she wanted to talk about her mother for now.

I jumped with a start. "Oh, I forgot her outside. She's probably got icicles hanging from her whiskers!"

Emily ran from the room and down the stairs. She had to save Girl. She threw open the back door and there was Girl, wagging her tail as if she didn't know it was thirty degrees. Emily grabbed her collar and pulled her inside, wrapping her arms around Girl's neck to help warm her.

"She needs hot chocolate," Emily said.

I handed her a bowl of dog food. "Let's start with this and see how she is after that." Emily picked up a handful of dog food and opened her palm for Girl. Emily wiped the crumbs from her hand onto her pajamas and followed me into the kitchen.

"Good morning, Emily," Mom said. "And merry Christmas!"

Emily sat at the island and watched Mom work. "Are we going to see the activity today?" Mom and I looked at her.

"What activity?" I asked, washing my hands.

"With all the animals and Mary and Joseph."

Mom threw her head back and laughed. "Oh! The *living* activity," she said.

"We'll do whatever you want," I said. I scrambled an egg and put a piece of toast on a plate for Emily. I poured her a glass of milk and set it in front of her. I was getting good at this.

"Can we go to see Mia today and can I buy her a gift for Christmas?"

"Yes, we can go see her."

"Can Mark go, too?" I knew Mom was waiting to hear my answer but she acted as if she were as busy as could be finishing the pie.

"We can ask. I'm sure he'll want to."

When Mark and Dad returned from shopping, a huge topiary entered the kitchen before Dad. "We're going to set this on the floor next to the mantle," he said. "What'd that lady call this thing, Mark?"

"A topiary."

Dad shook his head. "It looks better than it sounds. See, it's got real fruit mixed in with the artificial leaves. That way you can use it every year." He smiled and Mom laughed. For years we'd only heard him use construction and building terms. Today he was an article straight out of *Better Homes and Gardens.* Mark followed carrying large paper bags with handles. Emily drank the last of her milk and ran into the dining room to help. I searched for our camera in the hall closet and tried to snap a picture of Mom but the batteries were dead.

It's been four years, I thought, realizing the last time we'd used the camera. I popped new batteries into place, put in a roll of film, and stepped into the door of the dining room. I took a picture of Emily burrowing through the bags, of Mark and Dad hanging garland, of Dad giving me a thumbs-up while he strung some lights, of Mark helping Emily spread out the table runner, and of Mom licking her fingers and giving me a dirty look. We baked and cleaned and spruced up the house for our visitors and for the first time in years it felt normal; it felt real.

Mom and Dad left and Mark carried games in from the garage. "I bought these today," he said to Emily and me. He was holding Candy Land, and Chutes and Ladders. "Does anybody want to play?"

Emily held up her hand. "I do. But can we see Mia first?" She walked over to him and looked up. "Can you go with us?"

"I can't be seen in public with someone wearing reindeer pajamas," he said. Emily ran up the stairs into the bedroom, leaving Mark and me alone in the kitchen.

"The dining room is gorgeous," I said, breaking the silence. "Thanks for doing that."

He nodded. "Thanks for cooking."

"Mom did most of it. She's a much better cook than I am."

"Guess it depends on who you're asking,"

he said. He smiled and I wanted to hug him but I couldn't. He couldn't either. Roy was wrong. We didn't know what to do. There was something broken and neither of us knew how to fix it.

Emily ran downstairs and I helped her with her coat. "Are you coming to the activity tonight?" she asked Mark.

Mark raised an eyebrow and looked at her. "What activity?"

"The live one," she said, pulling on her gloves.

"The living Nativity," I said.

"You have to go because all the animals will be there," Emily said. "Mary and Jesus, too."

"Well, of course I'll go," he said, opening the car door for her. I sat next to her in the backseat.

"I love animals," she said. I knew she did from the way Girl responded to her. "We had a cat named Harry once, but he ran away."

"I have an uncle named Harry," I said. "We always wanted him to run away but he never did." Mark laughed out loud and his sudden outburst made me laugh. I caught him looking at me in the rearview mirror and when I saw him he smiled. I wasn't sure if he was smiling at me or because of what I had said. Did it matter? He was smiling again. And so was I.

We walked into the room where Mia was being monitored and Emily ran to her side. She was awake. "Hello, sweet girl," I said, stroking her hand with my finger. She smiled and Emily wrapped her hand around Mia's.

"Merry Christmas, Mia," she said. "We're going to see the animals tonight. I wish you could come with us." She made faces at Mia and Mia giggled. Emily beamed. She was so proud. She reached into a bag and pulled out the tinsel and strand of lights she'd brought for Mia's room. Mark plugged the lights in and formed them in a snake shape on the windowsill and wrapped the tinsel around Mia's bed where she couldn't reach it.

" 'Jingle bells, jingle bells, jingle all the way.' " Emily was singing. She looked up at Mark and me and nodded her head, trying to get us to sing as well. We looked around, hoping no one could hear, and joined in, whispering. "Louder," Emily said. We sang louder and Mia kicked her feet. " 'In a one-horse ohhh-penn sleiiighh,' " we all sang, giving the song a big finish. Fortunately, Dr. Andrews entered the room after the song was through.

He walked to Mark and extended his hand. "I'm Nathan Andrews."

"I'm Mark. Nice to meet you."

"She's doing great," he said, touching Mia's leg.

"Everything's working?" I asked, looking at the wires surrounding her.

"Everything's doing exactly what it's supposed to do."

"Will she ever be sick again?" Emily asked.

He put his hand on her shoulder. "I think Mia's going to surprise us all," he said. "And I love surprises. Especially at Christmas." He handed me an envelope and I opened it. It was full of money.

"What's this?" I asked.

"Somebody started a collection for Mia. We thought maybe you'd know what to do with it. You can use it however she needs it most." I felt like a little girl again watching Pastor Burke hand my mother an envelope at Christmas.

"This is so kind of everyone," I said, wishing I were better with words. "I can't believe they did this." He smiled and I knew that Mia wasn't the first child Dr. Andrews and the staff had rallied around at Christmas.

"Are you ready for Christmas?" he asked Emily. She shrugged but kind of grinned.

"Are you?" I asked.

"Oh, yes. My dad and his wife and my grandmother are coming to visit us this year because my wife is so pregnant that everyone's afraid she won't be able to make the trip to see them. They say they're coming to see us but I know they're hoping she has the baby early."

"When is she due?" I asked.

"The first of January."

"How long have you been married?"

"Three years tonight!"

We got out a round of congratulations before Dr. Andrews was paged to another room.

"If I don't see you again today, Emily," he said, kneeling in front of her, "I hope you enjoy this Christmas and every one after it."

She put her arms around his neck and hugged him. When everyone left, Emily pulled the gift she had chosen at the department store out of the bag. Mark and I had followed her earlier as she went from one floor to the next looking for the perfect present. It was sitting alone on a shelf that had long been picked over and emptied. She fluffed the angel's dress and set it on the windowsill by Mia's bed and then leaned in and whispered something to her. I kissed my finger and put it on Mia's head and then Emily did the same.

"I suppose you're not going to tell me what you said to Mia this time either," I said.

"I told her that her angel would stay with her until we got back. She can't see her angel. That's why I wanted to get her one, so she'd know what angels looked like."

Nathan Andrews walked past the nurses' station on the way to his office. "Are there any messages for me?"

A nurse looked at the message caddy next to her phone and shook her head. He walked toward his office, disappointed that he hadn't heard from Rory yet.

"Oh, wait, Dr. Andrews, you do have a message."

He turned around.

"Sorry. It was sitting on the desk instead of in the message carrousel." She picked it up and held it in front of her. It says, 'Found the needle.' That's all."

Nathan smiled. He went to his office and picked up the phone.

"Sorry, Dr. Lee had to go off site," someone said. "Some sort of explosion. He's already been gone close to an hour."

"Do you know if he left any sort of message to give to Nathan Andrews?"

The woman shuffled through paperwork

and grunted. "No, nothing here," she said. "I expect them to roll back in here any minute."

Nathan asked her to remind Dr. Lee to call him but he wasn't hopeful. Nathan jotted a name down on a notepad on his desk: "Mark." He underlined it. Then he wrote "Mark and Patricia Addison." He tried to put a face to the mother he had spoken to four years earlier but there was no use; he couldn't. It was part of his job that he didn't like; how names and faces could blur. For all he knew he was confusing everything in his mind: the young man, the mother, the gift, the social worker he'd met who had a deceased son. *Coincidence?* he thought. What were the odds? *Slim,* he thought, pushing away from the desk. In five hours he'd be eating dinner with his family. If Rory didn't call before then he'd forget about it till after Christmas.

After we returned home from the hospital Mark and Emily made a fire. When it crackled and popped and a steady flame wrapped around a log we sat together at the kitchen table and ate lunch. It was the first time Mark and I had sat at that table with someone else in four years. After lunch Mark sat on the sofa to read through the instructions for Candy Land. It had been so many years that neither one of us could remember how to play. He threw his legs up on the ottoman and Emily sat down next to him. Within minutes of Mark reading the instructions out loud she was asleep, falling over onto his shoulder. He tried to reach the blanket on the back of the sofa and I grabbed it, pulling it over her. "You may be there for a while," I said, whispering.

"I hope so," he said, wrapping his arm around Emily's shoulder and resting his hand on her arm. In a few short days Emily had managed to wrap Mark around her little finger. I guess she'd done that to both of us. It was going to be hard to place her in a foster home. I put the thought out of my mind. I didn't want to think about that right now. I'd deal with it after Christmas; then maybe it wouldn't be so hard. I looked at Mark. His head was resting on the back of the sofa and his eyes were closed. For so many years he hadn't been able to sit and relax. He had kept himself busy; we both had. I never took the time to rest because that paved the way for thinking and remembering, and those were painful options, especially if I wasn't ready for some of the memories. Emily repositioned herself and snuggled closer to Mark's side. He was relaxed now and the look on his face told me he was at peace. I didn't know if placing Emily was going to be harder on him or me.

At five o'clock we loaded into the car to go see the living Nativity. We picked Mom and Dad up and they were wearing matching red turtlenecks with green cardigans. They looked like a singing Christmas duo that might perform at nursing homes. Mom's sweater had a big Santa pin that said "ho, ho, ho" when you pulled his feet. Mark drove up the winding drive that led to Longworth Farm and noticed the man signaling him at the end of the field that had become the parking lot. The field was full of cars. Emily took Mark's hand and then mine and pulled us forward toward the entrance. I'd never seen a child so excited to see a few animals. Mom and Dad ran behind us to keep up. Emily dragged us past a man selling sugarcoated pecans and roasted cashews and a woman selling hot chocolate and cider. The barns on the property had enormous lit stars on each roof and swags of spruce that hovered above the barn's opening. Carolers dressed in Victorian costumes sang at the entrance of one barn while another was filled with a small petting zoo that included sheep, goats, ponies, and calves, each wearing a red Christmas ribbon and bell around its neck. Emily ran from one animal to another stroking its nose or patting its side. Mom snapped pictures of her with each animal, taking so many pictures that she had to change film.

We walked out of the barn and saw lines of people waiting for the horse-drawn sleigh rides. "This is just like a winter wonderland," Mom said, gasping at the sight of the sleighs gliding over the snowy meadow. I pulled Emily's hood over her head and zipped her coat as we waited our turn but she didn't seem to mind the chilly breeze. When our turn arrived, Mark and Emily and I sat in the front seat of the sleigh and Mom and Dad sat behind us. The driver clacked his tongue and the two black horses pulling our sleigh headed across the meadow, the bells around their necks jingling as they ran. Emily squealed and grabbed for my hand and Mark's, holding our hands in her lap. She was beside herself when the horses pulled us through the woods.

"We're going into the forest like Snow White," she said, looking wide-eyed around her. We passed a large gingerbread house with a waving gingerbread man out front and she popped up out of the seat. "Look," she said, pointing. "We could eat that!" She put her hands up to her mouth and pretended to bite and make chewing sounds. Mark laughed and eased her back down. She clapped and stomped her feet and Mom snapped one picture after another. The ride was over much too soon. Mark helped Emily out of the sleigh and then offered his hand to me. I accepted it and he helped me to the ground. I know Mom and Dad saw us but they pretended not to notice. They'd gotten just as good at pretending as Mark and I had.

We heard the music of a small orchestra and walked toward the largest barn in the distance where the Nativity was held. Large pine trees were decorated with white lights and an enormous star, bigger than those on the other barns, lit up the tin roof. "Wow," Emily said, stopping us. From where we were standing we couldn't see Mary or Joseph or any of the animals inside the barn because of the crowd in front of us. I noticed a spot opening up and moved toward it.

"Come up here," I said, leading the way.

Emily turned toward Mark, and without asking, Mark knew that she wanted to be lifted onto his shoulders. Bright lights shone on shepherds and a small shepherd boy who wandered about with some sheep and lots of donkeys, cows, goats, and even a camel. When the menagerie moved out of the way we could see Joseph and Mary and the little Baby Jesus. The music was soft now, a lullaby. I pointed to Mary holding a wriggling baby and Emily smiled. She hadn't expected to see such a small baby in the manger. Then the sky lit up and we looked to see five glowing angels hovering over the barn. The angel in front had long brown hair and a flowing crimson robe with delicate ribbons of gold. Music swelled as the angels opened their arms to the scene below them.

"There she is!" Emily shouted, pointing to the angel. "That's her!" Mark and I exchanged glances. Emily couldn't take her eyes off the angel. Three wise men dressed in elaborate costumes rode through the center of the crowd on camels and made their way to the barn but Emily didn't pay attention to them. "Look at her! Look how beautiful she is!"

"She is beautiful," I said.

Emily looked at Mom and Dad and pointed to the angel for them to see. "I couldn't see her because it was dark in my room. All I could feel was her hand." Mark looked at me and we knew she was talking about the night her mother died. He put

Emily down and I knelt in front of her.

"An angel held your hand, Emily?"

She nodded.

"Didn't that scare you when you felt someone's hand in the darkness?"

She looked at me as if I couldn't understand anything. "Angels aren't scary," she said. "They're nice. She held my hand and another angel held my mom's hand." That threw me for a moment.

"How do you know an angel held your mom's hand?"

She was getting exasperated with me. "Because that's what they do. They always watch us. When we die God sends an angel to hold our hand so we won't be afraid. Then when we die we float up to heaven with that angel." I could see Mom wipe her eyes. It's what she had told me four years ago after Sean's accident. The story of the angel was helping Emily with her mother's death and I wasn't about to change that. She needed to get through the grief in her own way. I took her hand and started walking toward the parking area. "Don't you believe me, Patricia?" Her voice was small, not as strong as it had been earlier. "Don't you believe that God sent my angel?" I searched her eyes. She believed everything she had told me.

"Yes," I said, pulling her toward me. "I believe you." She reached for Mark's hand and we walked in silence to the car.

Meghan Andrews put the last of the roast into a glass dish and covered it with Saran Wrap. Nathan's grandmother came up behind her and moved her out of the kitchen. "You cooked for us. Now we clean. Sit down before that baby decides to pay us all a visit on Christmas Eve. And you know what will happen if the baby comes too early?"

Nathan kissed his grandmother's cheek. "We know, Gramma," reciting the old wives' tale she'd told him for the past nine months. "If a baby comes early it'll be slow to walk and slower to talk."

"That's right. Your grandpa came early and he was nearly four years old before he talked."

"Maybe he didn't have anything to say. Maybe he was the strong, silent type."

"Your grandfather couldn't keep silent if you paid him!"

Nathan laughed and helped his grandmother clear the table.

"What I would give for this baby to come," Meghan said, sitting at the table. "I can hardly breathe anymore."

Jack smiled and helped clear the table. He didn't say it but Nathan knew his dad was anxious to meet his first grandchild.

Lydia held her hand on Meghan's stomach. "Oh, my goodness. We've got a little one who's excited about Christmas in there." Lydia had married Jack four years earlier. Nathan wished his own mother could meet his children and be called Grandma by little ones who clamored to get onto her lap but he had realized a long time ago that that would never happen. Lydia would be the baby's grandma. She had grandchildren already and was a good grandma. Nathan and Meghan knew she would love their child as one of her own as well.

When the dishes were finished, everybody sat in the living room by the tree and continued to talk about work, family, old friends, and the new baby. At nine o'clock the phone rang and Nathan answered it.

"Just another holiday in the ER." It was Rory.

"Are you still standing?"

"Barely. I have something for you."

Nathan walked to the closet and pulled the timepiece out of his pocket.

"There was a Sean Addison brought in four years ago on Christmas Eve."

Nathan looked at the inscription on the watch. "Mom, Always . . . S."

"Did anyone happen to record his personal items?" Nathan asked.

"No, there's nothing listed."

Nathan sighed. He knew it had been too much to hope for. He closed his hand around the pocket watch. "I owe you one."

"Actually, you owe Stephanie in Records. She did all the work." Nathan wished Rory a merry Christmas and hung up the phone. He sat on the sofa and wanted to share the story with the rest of his family but they were looking at Meghan's ultrasound pictures . . . again. He held the watch in his hands and shook his head. What if the watch didn't belong to the young man who had died that night in the ER? The *S* on the watch might not mean Sean. It could be for a Steven or Sarah or Susan. What if he gave this to Patricia Addison and she thought he was crazy? He had to be at the hospital early tomorrow; he could leave the watch on the Addison's front porch without their knowing and if it didn't belong to Patricia then she'd just assume someone left it at the wrong house. But with that settled, the question still nagged him: what if he was mistaken? He rubbed his thumb over the engraving on the watch, then put it in his shirt pocket, propped his feet up on the coffee table, and smiled. It wouldn't be the first time he was wrong.

Eight

The word which God has written on the brow of every man is Hope.
— Victor Hugo

I opened my eyes at six. It was Christmas morning and for the first time in years I didn't feel any sense of dread. I felt joy. But that couldn't be possible, not given Emily's situation or mine and Mark's. How could I feel such excitement about today? I leaned up on the bed and looked at Emily. *Please open the doors of a beautiful home for her with parents who will be crazy about her. Help her to enjoy today. Somehow. Some way.* I tiptoed out of the room and headed for the bathroom. I wanted to shower before everyone got there to watch Emily open her presents. Mark had put them under the tree last night after she had gone to bed. I turned the water on in the shower but thought I heard the doorbell. It couldn't be. Not at this hour. I thought I heard it again and turned off the water. Nothing. If it was the doorbell I assumed Mark would have heard it, too. I showered and got ready for the day before heading to the living room to plug in the tree. It was gorgeous. I found the camera so I'd be sure to have it with me as Emily opened her presents. I went to the kitchen, put the turkey in the oven, and started to peel sweet potatoes when I heard a door open upstairs. Girl's nails clicked on the hardwood floor at the top of the landing. "Patricia." I put down the knife and walked to the stairs. Emily and Girl were standing at the top resembling a picture on a Christmas card. Emily's hair looked as if it had been teased and ratted during the night and one of the legs of her pajamas was halfway up her calf. She held Ernie as Girl stood next to her, wagging her tail. "Is it Christmas?"

"It sure is," I yelled, throwing open my arms. "Merry Christmas!"

Mark came out of the hall bathroom dressed and ready for the day. "Merry Christmas," he yelled. Girl barked and ran down the stairs. Mark picked Emily up and ran down the stairs, showing her the tree.

Her jaw dropped. "Did Santa come?"

"He sure did," Mark said.

"He knew I was here?"

"Just take a look."

He set her down and she walked to the tree, looking at the names on the gifts. "That's my name," she said, looking for the tag on each present. "They're for me. He did know I was here. I don't believe it!"

I sat down next to her on the floor. "Greta and Hal really want to be here as you open your gifts. Can you wait thirty minutes?"

She shook her head.

"Can you wait twenty-five minutes?"

She nodded.

I laughed and reached for the phone. "Are you up?" I asked Mom. "Because Emily's ready to open!"

I hung up the phone and dialed Greta and Hal. Hal answered again. "Are you up?" I said, louder than usual. "Are you up?" I was shouting this time.

Emily giggled.

Greta answered the phone. "Are you ready to unwrap gifts?" I asked.

"Oh, my, yes," she said. "Hal, go get your hearing aids in. Your hearing aids. Your ears." She was shouting into the phone. "Right. Go get them. We'll be over just as soon as I can get some pants on Hal. I've got everything ready."

Mark made a fire and put on a pot of coffee to brew. Emily didn't move from the tree. I was able to convince her to use the bathroom and wash her face and brush her teeth before everyone arrived. When she finished she took her place in front of the tree again. Within minutes the house was buzzing. Mom arrived carrying an enormous coffee cake loaded with nuts and raisins and gooey stuff that ran down the side of it. Greta arrived with a huge bowl of mixed fruit (to offset the calories and fat of the coffee cake). With coffee cups in hand we gathered in the living room. Emily couldn't wait any longer. She opened the Easy Bake oven first and her eyes popped out. "I've wanted this since I was little," she said. Greta and Hal had bought her a new winter coat. It was pink with large round pink buttons and fake white fur around the collar. She tried it on and looked like a tiny Audrey Hepburn. The books came next and she flipped through each one looking at the pictures and pretending to read. I looked at the faces in the room and realized it didn't matter that there wasn't a gift under the tree for any of us. This wasn't about us. Emily propped her new baby doll in the stroller and covered her with a little blanket. "I'll be done in a minute," she said to the doll. "Then we can play." I snapped a picture but Emily didn't notice. With each gift that was opened we all said "Ooh" and "Ahh" or "Wow, isn't that nice!" She opened the jewelry box from Roy and wound up the ballerina so she would dance for us. Emily put strands of beads around her neck and lined her wrist with dangly plastic bracelets. Roy was right again; she loved it. I took another picture and found myself smiling the whole time. I couldn't stop; neither could Mark. I hadn't seen him so excited in years. He handed her a small box and Emily shook it, wondering what was inside. She ripped into the paper and pulled out a small cross, covered with pink stones.

"That's from your mom," Greta said, watching her. Emily held it in her hands and stared at it. She turned it over and saw there was engraving on the back.

"What does this say?"

Mark knelt down and looked over her shoulder. "It says, 'For Emily. Love, Mom.' And that word right there is 'Christmas.' "

She ran her finger over the writing. "Can you put it on me?" Mark took it from her and put it around her neck. She picked it up and looked at it.

"It's beautiful, Emily," Greta said. "It's just absolutely beautiful."

Emily didn't say anything but she nodded. One day she'd realize how special that little cross was. In the corner of my eyes I saw Mom brush a tear off her cheek. No one had expected a gift from Tracy but I was so glad Greta had found it. The Easy Bake oven and doll would last only for a little while but the necklace would be the gift that Emily would remember and keep for the rest of her life.

Mark looked to the back of the tree. "Here's the last one. Are you ready for it?"

Emily nodded. He handed it to her and she tore through the paper. She opened the top of the box and lifted tissue paper to see the princess dress.

She gasped and pulled it out of the box. "I told Santa I wanted this. This is my dress!" She pointed her foot and held it under her chin; then she swayed back and forth so she could see the layers of silk and crinoline flow.

Mark showed her the tiara and put it on her head, then pulled out the pair of sequined plastic shoes. Emily scrambled out of her pajamas and Mark slid the dress over her shoulders. "May I, Your Majesty?" he asked, holding one of the shoes in front of her.

She nodded and he helped her into both

shoes. We all said "Aww" at the same time and she twirled for us. Hal clapped the loudest and Mom and Greta said over and over that she was more beautiful than either Snow White or Cinderella. I snapped several pictures in a row. Emily was beside herself. I didn't know how long her happiness would last or when the sadness of her life would sneak up on her again but in that moment she was happy and so were Mark and I. I didn't know how I could feel a sense of contentment in the middle of this tragedy but I did.

It was over too soon. Greta bent down to wad up discarded wrapping paper. "It's okay, Greta," I said. "Just leave it." If we cleaned everything up it would mean that the morning was slipping away and I wanted to hold on to it as long as I could. Mark and Hal helped Emily set up the Easy Bake oven while Mom, Greta, and I put coffee cake and fruit onto plates.

"Thank you again for inviting us," Greta said. "She means the world to us."

"She means the world to us, too," I said, before realizing it. Mom didn't react; she just licked her fingers and made yummy noises before picking a plate for Dad and carrying it into the living room. Emily wanted to visit Mia in the hospital before she started playing with her new toys. "I didn't think we'd visit today since we were just there yesterday afternoon," I said.

"We have to go," Emily said. "It's Christmas and she'll know she's alone." I thought maybe just the women would go but before I knew it, we had all piled into Mark's SUV and Mom and Dad's car for the short trip to the hospital. Mia was awake. When she saw Emily she smiled. Emily stuck a finger into Mia's palm and gently bounced it up and down.

" 'Silent night, holy night.' " Oh, no, she was singing again. Her voice was small and sweet. She looked at us hoping we'd join in as we had yesterday, and we did. Mom and Dad moved closer and joined us. They waved Hal and Greta over and there we stood, a ragtag group of carolers singing to a tiny heart patient on Christmas Day. " 'Sleep in heavenly peace,' " we sang, trying to harmonize as best we could. " 'Sleep in heavenly peace.' "

We cheered for ourselves when we hit the last note and Greta started the next song. " 'Hark the herald angels sing,' " she began, searching for a note. Mom and I attempted to help her out. " 'Glory to the newborn king!' " Hal tried to clap but it clearly wasn't working. Greta grabbed his hands so we could finish and what a finish it was! Mark took the low note, Mom attempted the high one, and the rest of us just kind of jumped in and hung on as best we could. It was lousy but wonderful. I hadn't sung in years. Someone began to clap behind us.

"How much can we pay you to entertain the whole unit?"

We turned to see Dr. Andrews.

"We'll do it if you take the solos," I said.

He held up his hand. "I knew early on that I had a voice for medicine, not singing."

"You don't even get a day off for Christmas?" I asked.

"I got here at the crack of dawn. I don't have a long day. And it's gotten a whole lot better seeing Emily this morning and hearing that beautiful singing."

We laughed, embarrassed at our lack of musical ability and wished him a Merry Christmas. We needed to get home; it was time to eat.

That was one of the best days I can remember. We played games with Emily and Mom and Greta and I worked together in the kitchen to prepare the meal. Emily sat at the head of the table wearing her princess dress and then we all joined hands and Dad thanked God for the food, for Christ's birth, and for new friends. We ate and laughed and played another game and ate some more, then went for a walk to the woods and ate even more. Though there were three men in the house we never turned the TV on to watch football or catch sports highlights of any kind. Somehow, without saying a word, we were all unified in making the day special for Emily. We listened to Hal tell stories of his childhood and Dad laughed so hard tears ran down his face. Emily didn't understand half the stories but she laughed anyway, mostly at us. She served cake from the Easy Bake oven and though everyone was full to the brim, we each took a bite. Mark kept the fire going throughout the day and at eight o'clock when it was dying down Hal and Greta got up to leave. I couldn't believe the day was over.

Greta leaned down and hugged Emily to her. "Merry Christmas, darlin'," she said, kissing her face. She hugged her so tight Emily caught her breath. I know that Greta worried that she'd never see her again. "I sure do love you," she said.

Emily patted her back. "I love you, too, Greta."

Hal got down on his knees and looked at Emily. "Can I get a peck right here?" he said, pointing to his cheek. Emily wrapped her arms around Hal's neck and kissed him hard on the cheek. "Thanks for letting us spend Christmas with you."

Emily nodded and wrapped her arm around his leg.

"You come see us anytime you can." Hal's voice started to break and Greta turned away. They didn't want to cry. Not now. Greta kissed Emily again and they waved at Mark and me as they walked out the door.

Dad helped Mom with her coat and she sat down at the kitchen table in front of Emily. "Merry Christmas, Emily. I can't remember meeting someone that I've liked more."

Emily smiled and Mom pulled her closer, kissing her head.

Dad extended his hand and Emily shook it like a big girl. "I've met a lot of fairy princesses in my life but you're the sweetest, and by far you're the prettiest."

Emily moved to my side, embarrassed. We said our good-byes and they walked to their car. I hated to see them go.

I sat at the table and pulled Emily onto my lap. "You were the belle of the ball," I said. "Are you tired?"

She shook her head.

"Would you like to take a bubble bath?"

"Can Girl come, too?"

I set her down. "She can't get in the tub,"

I said. "She'll eat up all the bubbles!" Emily and Girl started up the stairs as I put the last few things into the refrigerator.

"It was a great day, Patti." I turned to see Mark standing at the island. He hadn't called me Patti in years.

"It was," I said, smiling. "I think she had a good time. All things considered."

"I did, too," he said. "It was a great Christmas." Emily called me from the bathroom and Mark moved in next to me. "Go ahead. I'll finish here."

By the time I walked into the bathroom Emily had bubbles up to her chin. Girl was up on her hind legs dipping her nose into the tub trying to move the bubbles away. Her head was covered and I laughed when I saw her. "She *is* trying to eat the bubbles," Emily said, trying to push Girl away. Girl jumped up and stuck her head right in the center of the tub again.

I yelled for Mark to bring the camera. He brought it in and snapped pictures of Girl looking as if her head was missing because it was buried beneath the foam, of Emily wearing bubbles on top of her head like a big frothy hat, and of Emily pushing Girl away before she jumped into the tub completely. It took forever to get the suds to go down the drain. I had to rinse Emily's body off before I helped her out of the tub. I wrapped a towel around her and she laid her head on my shoulder. I hugged her and felt my heart flutter. How did I let myself get attached to this child? I combed her hair and blew it dry and then helped her into her pajamas.

"We should take your necklace off before you go to bed," I said.

She wrapped her hand around it. "Where will you put it?"

I laid it on the dresser. "Right here. We'll put it back on first thing in the morning." She watched as I laid it on the top of the dresser. I helped her into bed and leaned down to kiss her face. "Thank you for being here for Christmas."

She nodded and nestled into the pillow, holding Ernie and her new baby doll. She looked at me and grinned.

"I better get Mark up here so he can kiss you good night, too."

I pulled the covers up onto her chest and she grabbed my hand. "Thank you, Patricia." I kissed her all over her face before I called Mark. I walked toward the door and Girl jumped off the bed, following me. "Can she stay?" Emily asked.

"I think she might need to go outside," I said. "I'll let her out and then she can come sleep with you."

Mark said good night while I opened the back door for Girl. I was unloading the dishwasher when Girl started to bark at something out front. I knocked on the front kitchen windows and she stopped. I put glasses into the cabinet but then heard Girl barking again. I walked to the front door and called her before she disturbed the neighbors. She ran up the front steps and I noticed a bag hanging on the doorknob. *What in the world?* I thought. The card attached to it said "Patricia." I couldn't imagine who had left it there.

I stepped inside the door and took the bag into the living room. I dug through the gold tissue paper and found a tiny note folded on top of a gift wrapped in delicate green foil paper. It read "Found at the hospital." My mind couldn't process things fast enough. Did I leave something at the hospital when I was visiting Mia? I ripped into the paper and discovered a black velvet box. I lifted the lid and saw a beautiful antique pocket watch with elaborate engraving. *What in the world?* I thought again, trying to figure out who would have given me such a beautiful gift. I turned the watch over and discovered engraving on the back. *"Mom, Always . . . S."*

I gasped and fell onto the sofa. A note card with a gold embossed heart at the top was in the bottom of the box. I began to cry when I recognized Sean's handwriting.

Dear Mom,

You always told me that the best Christmas gift I could ever give was the one I couldn't wrap — the gift of time. That never made sense until I got older and saw how you gave your time to "your kids," and to Dad and me. And I noticed that you never just gave your time at Christmas, Mom. You gave it away every day — 24/7.

At the very first Christmas, angels said, "I bring you good news of great joy for everyone!" When I was little you told me that the good news was that God loves everyone (so much that He sent His Son to live here). A lot of people don't know about God's love but I know about it every time you hug me (how's that for mushy?!). And every time I see you hug one of "your kids" I know they feel it, too. (Okay, enough mush. I need to move on!)

You said your grandfather's watch was "just a thing" but I know it was more than that to you: every time you looked at it you remembered time spent with him or the time you spend with Grandma. You warned me (lectured is more like it!) to be careful how I spent my time because before I knew it the day would be gone. So before another day and another Christmas got away I wanted to give this to you and thank you for being the best mom in the world and for giving me the gift of your time every day. I know you have to unwrap this, but in a way I'm giving you the gift of more time that we'll be able to spend together!

I love you, S

Mark ran down the stairs and discovered me on the sofa. Tears streamed down my face as I held the watch and note for him to see. He took the watch from me and read the note. He was stunned. He read the note again and looked back at the inscription on the watch. It didn't make sense. How could this be from Sean? He looked at the note and watch again.

"Who left this?" he asked.

I shook my head.

"How did they even know it was you or Sean or . . ." His voice started shaking and he sat down next to me.

"I thought I heard the doorbell ring this

morning when I was in the shower but with everyone here I forgot all about it," I said. "I'm sure it's been there all day." I cried harder and held the watch close to me. Mark pulled me to him and I wrapped my hand tighter around the watch. I never wanted to let it go. "I miss him every single day," I said. Mark wrapped his arms around me and I felt his tears on the back of my neck. "It's gotten to the point where I can't hear his voice anymore and I'm so afraid I won't remember what he sounded like. I won't remember what he sounded like when he'd run through the door and say, 'Hey, Mom. What's up?' I won't remember what he sounded like when he'd say, 'I love you.' And I don't ever want to forget."

"You won't," Mark said, wiping my face. "You won't forget." He walked into the kitchen and brought back a tiny cassette and the answering machine. He placed the cassette inside the machine, sat down on the sofa next to me, and pushed Play. It was Sean's last message home on the night he died. I closed my eyes and tears streamed over my lips, into my mouth.

"Hey, Mom, I'm on the road," he said. "I left an hour ago so I'll see you in a couple more. I'm going to be losing cell service in a few minutes but call if you need me. See you in a little while. Love ya." *See you in a little while.* Time would pass *so* quickly for Sean.

We both sat and cried as Mark played the message over and over. It was the first time we had really grieved together. Mark handed me a tissue and I wiped my face. My head pounded; it had been an exhausting few days. "He loved you, Patti," Mark said. "Sean always loved you." I twisted a soggy tissue in my hand and smiled. "Do you think God parted the clouds today so Sean could see us?"

"I think he probably did."

Mark was quiet. "Sean's Christmases have been a whole lot better than ours."

"I know," I said, holding the tissue on my eyes.

"He's waiting for us, Patti."

I leaned my head on the back of the sofa and nodded.

"*Did* God send an angel to hold her hand?" He was thinking of what Emily had said at Longworth Farm.

"Yes," I said. "I believe her."

"Was an angel holding her mother's hand?"

I shrugged. I couldn't and didn't want to answer because I knew where Mark was leading.

"Was an angel holding Sean's hand?" I wanted to hold back the tears but there was no use in trying. "Did an angel hold him at the end?" I began to sob and Mark pulled me in to him. My head throbbed but was reeling with so many questions. Is death God's final act of mercy in our lives? Does He send an angel to help us through our last seconds on earth? Does He send an angel to hold the hand of a frightened child who's waiting for her mother, who will never return home? Did an angel go through Sean's accident with him? "He wasn't afraid," the young doctor said that night. "He was calm as he spoke to me. Everything about him was peaceful." Was it God's presence that had given Sean that peace?

"I love you, Patti," Mark said. He held my arms and looked at me. "If I could bring Sean back I would, but I can't do that. I don't want to lose you, too, but I don't know what to do anymore. I don't know what you want or what I can do to help you. All I know is that I have never stopped loving you, Patti."

I closed my eyes and sobbed. Mark was a good man. He had always been a good, kind, and decent man but I somehow managed to drive him away. I looked at him and saw the same handsome face that had smiled at me after he spilled spaghetti all over me so many years ago.

"Why did you stay?" I asked.

He looked up at the ceiling. "Because I took these crazy vows and the minister made me believe that they were real!" I smiled. "Let me tell you, nobody would repeat those things if they knew the anguish, turmoil, grief . . . and happiness that came with them."

I tried to laugh but cried harder.

He took hold of my shoulders again. "Do you love me?" He had to ask because for years I hadn't given him any reason to believe that I did.

"Yes," I said, so quiet I was certain he hadn't heard me. But he had. He leaned over and kissed me. I pulled away and looked at him. How could we have been lost for so long? We walked upstairs and I opened Emily's door so Girl could take her place at the foot of the bed. Emily was asleep. Mark and I walked into our bedroom, closed the door, and talked into the night. I doubted I would ever know who rang our doorbell that day but I knew enough: four years after Sean's death God had sent two angels to me at Christmas to save my life. One had given me a gift from my son, and the other, a five-year-old named Emily, had given me reason to hope and to teach me about my son's death: God wasn't a liar. He was with Sean to the end, just as He promised.

Roy was right; it was time to live again.

NINE

Hope and fear are inseparable.
— François de la Rochefoucauld

"Isn't there anything we can do?" Mark asked.

I shook my head. "She has to be with a foster family."

"How long would it take for us to become a foster family? We could hurry up and do it and then she could stay with us till she's adopted."

"There is no hurry up and do it," I said. "It takes three months." There was nothing we could do. We'd been up through the night trying to find a way for Emily to stay with us but there wasn't one. I turned on my Palm Pilot and found the phone number for a foster family I'd worked with many times over the years and called them. Yes, they would take Emily. I hung up the phone and looked at Mark. How could we give up a child that we loved? I had to go to the office and begin the paperwork. I hadn't been to the office since I picked her up and I needed to file the necessary papers. I couldn't put it off any longer. I hoped to be home by the time Emily was awake. "When I'm finished I'll call and you'll need to bring her to the office." I got my coat and Mark took it from me, kissing me. Throughout the night I knew why I had brought Emily home with me; God had enabled her visit to bring Mark and me back together. But what did that mean for Emily? What would happen to her? Those questions weighed on me as I drove to work.

There were a few people in the office who were pretending to be busy but they were mostly talking about what they did for Christmas. I avoided them and went to my desk to prepare Emily's file. *You've done this for years,* I thought. *Just do it and get it over with.* I pulled out the forms and began to file my report, filling in all the necessary blanks: *Deceased, orphan, five years old, no legal guardian, foster home.* I stopped writing and shook my hand. It felt as if I were moving a twenty-pound pen around on the page. I typed into my computer about the night I was called to take Emily into protective services and meeting the police at her home before reporting the phone call from Karen Delphy and explaining their situation. I stared at the words on the screen: December 21. Had it only been five days ago? The phone rang at my desk. I considered letting it ring but thought it might be Mark. I picked up the receiver.

"Patricia," a young voice said.

"Justin?" I thought, *Oh, please don't let anything be wrong.*

"We decorated a Christmas tree."

I sighed. "That's great, Justin. Is it pretty?"

"It's awesome," he said, describing it to me in detail. "You can come see it if you want."

I told him I would.

"I got a lot of cool presents, too, and my mom made a turkey."

"How is your mom?" I asked.

"She's cool," he said.

I was relieved. Justin and his mother were doing well. "Thanks for calling me," I said.

"I just wanted to wish you a late merry Christmas and tell you happy New Year, too," he said, mumbling into the phone. "And say . . . thanks for, uh . . . for bringing me back." He hung up before I could say anything. *There are still happy endings,* I thought, reminding myself.

"What in the world are you doing here?"

I jumped in my seat and spun around to see Roy.

"I have to file a report on Emily," I said, turning back to my computer. I should have asked how Roy's Christmas was but I couldn't. I didn't want to talk with anyone, not even Roy.

"Is she going into a foster home today?"

I nodded but kept working.

"How does she feel about that?"

I shrugged, keeping my back to him.

"How do you feel about that?"

I stopped typing. "I'm sick about it," I said. "But there's nothing we can do. You know that." I started to type again. I was determined to finish the report.

Roy tapped me on the shoulder. "Excuse me," he said.

I ignored him.

This time he tapped harder. "I said excuse me."

I rubbed my shoulder. "Ow! What are you doing?"

"I think the better question is what are *you* doing?"

"I'm trying to get this report ready."

He sat down on the edge of my desk. "Well, somebody might be able to help you if you'd just stop working for a second."

"Help me with what? I've done these reports a thousand times."

He sighed and threw his hands in the air. "You women drive me crazy. I don't know why I ever asked Barbara to marry me. Now I'll be having conversations like this for the rest of my life!"

I jumped out of my seat and hugged Roy. "You finally did it! Why didn't you tell me?"

"Tell you? You can't keep a secret. For days we planned a surprise birthday party for Glenda and she never had a clue until you blabbed."

"That was ten years ago!"

"It left a mark!" I sat in my chair and looked up at him. He was happy and proud.

"Is the ring pretty?"

He held his fingers in front of him and then pretended to shine them on his sleeve. "I don't like to brag but she cried when she saw it."

"Because the diamond was so small?"

He slapped the desk and laughed and then picked up the paperwork on my desk. I watched him read through it.

"How was Christmas?" I couldn't tell Roy everything; it would take too long.

"I hated to see it end." He shuffled the paperwork in his hands and studied what I'd written. He rested his forehead on his thumb and middle finger and read through each line again. I continued working but could hear Roy rustling the papers behind me.

After several minutes he rested the papers on his knee. "She has a living grandmother, grandfather, and uncle?"

"Yes."

"And none of them are legal guardians?" I didn't know what he was getting at.

"No."

"How do you know?"

"I called them the morning after the accident. None of them could take Emily."

"They couldn't take her. What does that mean exactly?"

His questions were beginning to annoy me and I gave Roy a frustrated look. "It means they couldn't take her," I said, this time with more emphasis.

"Did you *ask* if any of them were Emily's legal guardian, or did they *think* that you were calling to ask them to take on their legal guardian role and they were declining?"

I shot up in my seat. I finally knew what Roy was doing. I had been asking the same questions for years. How could I have forgotten to ask about legal guardians this time? I scrambled for the phone and picked up the receiver but realized I had to look up Greta's number first. I dug through my purse for my Palm Pilot. "Roy, what have I done? How could I forget to ask such a basic question?" I asked, emptying the contents of my purse out on my desk. "How could I forget? What does this mean?" He pressed my hand to stop me from moving.

"It means that if one of those relatives can't be the legal guardian that maybe they could name you and Mark as legal guardians until you find a permanent home for her." He smiled and I fell back into my seat.

"How did you know?"

"Do you think I'm blind? Anybody can see that that little girl has you all tied up in knots. You're not doing your job right, you're decorating Christmas trees, and you're dumping your purse out like a crazy person. I'm not the brightest guy in the world but after seventeen years I do notice some things."

I picked up the phone and dialed Greta's number. "Greta! I'm so glad you're home. Do you know if Tracy made anyone in her family the legal guardian of Emily?"

"I don't know. Why?" There was no time to explain everything.

"Do you know if Tracy had a lawyer at any time or if she had any important paperwork that she kept somewhere?"

"Let me think." She was silent and I waved my hand in the air toward Roy as if trying to hurry her. "Hal!" She was calling Hal. This could take all day. "Hal," she said, louder. "Did Tracy keep important paperwork anywhere? Did Tracy keep . . . hold on," she said into the phone. She covered the phone and yelled. I heard mumbling and the gurgling sound phones make when someone covers the receiver. Out of nerves I started to bounce my leg up and down. What in the world was taking so long? "He's got a whole box here filled with papers we found the day we cleaned Tracy's house. He didn't know if it was important or not so he brought it home."

"Don't go anywhere," I said to Greta. "I'm coming right over." I pushed everything back into my purse and ran down the hall toward the elevator. I turned to look at Roy. "Are you coming or not?" He grabbed his coat and ran after me. I thought I was going to explode. I had to call Mark. I picked up my cell phone but decided to wait. I couldn't get him excited, too. Not yet.

On the way to Greta's I told Roy everything that had happened. I told him the story of the watch and the note and he smiled ear to ear, listening. I rambled on and on about talking with Mark and listening to Sean's last voice message. Roy leaned over to look at the speedometer several times and checked his seat belt. I was driving as fast as I was talking. I ran through Greta's front door without knocking. The box was sitting on the kitchen table. I lifted the lid and it was chaos inside. Nothing was in files or in order. "Okay," I said, dumping it onto the table. "Here we go. Look for anything that resembles a will or papers with a law firm listed at the top of the page." Greta and Hal both reached for their glasses.

"Gas bill, electric bill, MasterCard," I said, throwing the papers to the floor.

"Here's something," Hal said. I jumped. "No, never mind. It's just a receipt from the guy who sold her her car." He studied the paper. "She never should have paid that much for that car. It wasn't worth that. Look at this, Greta."

"Hal," I said. "Please keep looking."

He threw the paper down and picked up another stack. One sheet after another fell to the floor. There were fewer and fewer pieces on the table. Disappointment was setting in. I looked at the remainder of papers in Hal's, Greta's and Roy's hands and knew they were only old bills. Nothing was here. Why did I let myself get so excited? I held a handful of papers in front of me and slumped into a kitchen chair. I handed them to Roy and he patted my shoulder, throwing the papers onto the table. Greta and Hal were quiet as they stared at them. Those papers were our last hope. I grabbed them and ran out the door.

Roy knocked on the door. No answer. He looked at the number on the paper and then to the door again, 4A. It was the right door. He balanced a cup of coffee in his hand and knocked louder. A man in his late twenties opened the door a crack and peered out at us. He was squinting from the light in the hallway. "Are you Randall Weist?" Roy asked.

"Who are you?" His voice was tired but defensive.

"We're with the Department of Family Services and need to talk to you about Tracy Weist."

He opened the door and we stepped inside to a living room. It was dark; the drapes were pulled and I doubted they'd been opened for weeks. It smelled musty from a combination of dirty laundry, empty beer cans and stale cigarettes. Roy handed him a cup of coffee and a bag of doughnuts we'd brought for him. Randall was in his underwear. He was tall and skinny; his ribs showed every time he took a deep breath. He pushed magazines to the side and asked if we wanted to sit down. A pair of jeans was draped over the arm of the sofa and he pulled them on, pushing the hair out of his eyes. Once he sat down in front of us I recognized him from the funeral.

"What about Tracy?" he asked.

"Randall," Roy said.

"It's Randy."

"I'm sorry. Randy. We've got papers here that we found in Tracy's things that indicate that you are Emily's legal guardian."

Roy handed him the papers and Randy looked through them, frowning. "I already told some lady that I couldn't take Emily."

I remained quiet. We had agreed on the drive here that Roy would do all the talking.

"Because of your work schedule?" Roy asked.

Randy looked at Roy and opened his arms. "Look at this place! I can't raise a kid. I don't want to raise a kid." His voice was getting pinched and tight.

"It's okay," Roy said. "We're not expecting you to raise her. We just want to make sure that you are indeed her legal guardian."

Randy didn't answer. He rubbed his head and looked at us. "Look, after Emily was born my sister called and asked if I'd take her kid in case anything happened to her and I said yes because I never expected anything to happen. I just did it because I knew that's what Tracy wanted me to say. I signed these papers because it helped her, that's all. I never knew anything would happen." I didn't say it but he'd made one of the best choices of his life the day he signed those papers. "I can't take her," he said again. "I can't do it."

"I can," I said, leaning in. We talked for forty-five minutes and in that time Randy ate all six of the doughnuts in the bag. He was relieved to know he wasn't legally bound to take Emily. We told him we'd call soon, and left. I walked into the hallway, leaned up against the wall, and exhaled.

"It's not over yet," Roy said. "Come on." Roy flipped open his cell phone and picked up the guardianship document we'd found in the box at Hal and Greta's. He began to call lawyers that we ran into on a consistent basis. No one was in their offices. I was getting worried. We needed a lawyer who could help us transfer legal guardianship to Mark and me. Roy called three more numbers with no luck.

I took the papers from Roy's hand and read the letterhead. "I'm going to call this firm," I said, handing him the papers.

"If lawyers aren't working in the city there's no way they're working in smaller places like Jefferson."

I held up my hand and dialed information. "This is for Jefferson," I said, waiting. "Yes, I need the number for a law firm called Layton and Associates." During the first year of Emily's life, Tracy had lived in Jefferson. She chose a lawyer based on location. She wanted one that was close to her brother's side of town so it would be easy for Randy to sign the papers. I was connected to the number. It began to ring. I paced the sidewalk in the front of Randy's apartment building, trying to break ice with the heel of my shoe. I let the phone ring and ring. No one was working. I was about to hang up when it clicked.

"Layton and Associates. This is Jodie."

"Hi," I said, surprised. "I didn't expect to get anyone today."

"I'm not supposed to be here," Jodie said. She was in a hurry. "I had to get a few files pulled together before I left town for New Year's. Normally we wouldn't be in." I sensed that Jodie answered the phone because she thought I was going to be someone else, like her boyfriend, and that she didn't want to be on the phone. I hurried through the situation, skipping over important details. She was quiet.

"You're sure that Robert Layton's name is on that paperwork?"

"I'm looking right at it."

"It's just that that work isn't something that Mr. Layton normally does, but he has taken a lot of pro bono cases over the years. This was probably one of them." She wasn't in a rush anymore. "You don't need us to put together paperwork, though. A lawyer closer to you can draw up the papers."

"We can't find a lawyer and we need one ASAP."

"How fast?" she asked.

"Now."

There was a brief pause. "Let me see what I can do." She put me on hold and within a couple of minutes the phone clicked.

"This is Robert Layton." I apologized for bothering Mr. Layton on vacation. I highlighted the story again: five-year-old orphan, mother killed in a car accident, legal guardianship rights. Could they be transferred?

"Is the brother alive?" Mr. Layton asked.

"We just met with him and he wants to

sign over his guardianship rights to another couple."

"And you need this done today?"

"I know it's a stretch," I said, "but we're going to have to uproot this little girl again and —"

"It's okay," Mr. Layton said, stopping me. "I'm happy to help." I gave Roy a thumbs-up. Mr. Layton was going to draft new paperwork and fax it to us for Randy's signature. "Can you give me thirty minutes? I need to boot up my computer here at home." I thought it would take him hours.

"Thirty minutes is great! Thank you, Mr. Layton. I hope you had a great Christmas." I hung up and knew I'd never talk to that lawyer again. I didn't know anything about him: his age, if he was married with kids or grandkids, or what kind of man he was, but I wondered if he would ever know what he had done or how he had helped. *God can use anybody or anything,* the minister had said so many Christmases ago. *Don't ever underestimate who or what He'll use to get something done.* We drove to an office supply store and waited for the fax. The cover page had my name and the words "Merry Christmas and Happy New Year!!!" It was turning out that both of those were ringing true.

Roy and I drove back to Randy's apartment and knocked several times before he answered. He'd been sleeping again. Poor guy. I know he was glad to see us leave once and for all. We got back in the car and Roy dialed Lynn McSwain's number.

"He's not going to be available the day after Christmas," I said.

"He's the supervisor," Roy said. "That's what supervisors do. They make themselves available on any day at any . . . Hello, Lynn," he said, glancing at me. "Patricia and I need to talk to you about something. . . . No, we need to do it today." I closed my eyes. I knew Lynn had a house full of relatives and he was going to try to put us off till later in the week. "We can be there in an hour and thirty minutes." Roy drove and this time we made the two-hour trip in a little over an hour.

We pulled into Lynn's driveway and I grabbed Roy's arm. I felt nervous and sick. "This is impossible," I said.

He patted my hand. "Keep things in perspective," he said. "This isn't impossible. Finding good cell service is impossible." Lynn opened the door before we knocked and we said hello to sons and daughters and grandchildren of all ages. Lynn led us into a small office and closed the door.

"What's up?" I didn't even know where to start but I told him about picking Emily up and taking her to Wesley House only to turn around and drive to our house instead. He held on to the ankle that was crossed over his knee and leaned on the desk, listening. He didn't interrupt; Lynn had always been a good listener. He didn't pull out papers to write me up for having a child at my house for five days, although I know the thought had to be in his mind. He remained quiet till I finished and then leaned back in his chair, pressing his hands together. "So this man is the child's uncle and legal guardian?" He held the papers in front of him.

I nodded.

"But you didn't know that?"

"I asked if he could take Emily but apparently I didn't ask if he was the legal guardian."

He was quiet again. He'd talk with me about how to do my job at another time. At that time he might even write me up for improper conduct and risking the life of a child by bringing her into my home. It was within his right to do it and I was sure he would.

"It was a mistake," Roy said. "But sometimes mistakes are good."

Lynn glanced at Roy and Roy stopped talking.

"So Randall Weist cannot take the child but will grant legal guardianship to someone who can take her in until she's adopted?"

"That's right," I said.

"Are the people Randall has in mind relatives of the child?"

"No, but they care for her very much."

"Have you been to the home?"

"Yes, I have. It's a lovely home with a big backyard and a dog that's crazy about Emily. The parents would provide a loving, stable home for her."

Lynn raised his eyebrow and looked at me. "Any other children?"

"No."

"And you somehow managed to find a lawyer to draft new paperwork today?"

I nodded.

"With signatures?"

I nodded again.

"Is this your home, Patricia?"

I bit my lip.

Lynn looked at Roy and then back at me. "Do you understand the needs this child is going to have?"

"I know loss, Lynn. I know what it's like to bury someone you love. Mark and I both know. The world looks different after that, people sound strange, TV doesn't make sense, losing twenty dollars or stubbing your toe in the middle of the night doesn't matter anymore because your heart doesn't beat the same. Everything changes. It's like nothing matters yet things matter more than they ever have because your soul has been ripped apart." I stopped. "No one understands that except those who've buried someone close to them. Mark and I have."

Lynn leaned back in his chair and sighed. If Emily was going to stay in our home then a few matters needed to be cleared up. "Who exactly is the social worker for this case?"

"I am," Roy said.

"As of?"

"Right now."

Lynn smiled.

"Can you think of any reasons why the courts wouldn't transfer rights to us as legal guardians?" I asked.

"Oh, I can think of several," Lynn said. I felt deflated. "I know you want to provide some stability for this child before she's adopted but the courts don't move that fast. You know that. They'll also see many variables as to why they shouldn't move in your favor but in favor of the foster system." It's astonishing how fast a promising situation can become hopeless but there was always a part of me that expected defeat. That way, when the rug was pulled out from underneath me I wouldn't be too upset or disappointed. I knew I couldn't expect a miracle at every turn but I at least wanted to try everything I could, and I did. I needed to be happy with that. Roy put his arm around me and helped me to the car. The wind was up; it had turned so cold.

I called Mark and asked if he would drive Emily to the office. I needed to get this over with so we could all get on with our lives. I looked out the window. It was snowing again. I watched for Mark to pull into the parking lot and then walked out the front doors of the building. I asked Mark if I could drive and he let me behind the wheel. I turned to look at Emily. She tried to smile but couldn't.

"Emily," I said, "I know you don't want to talk about this but can I at least drive you to the home you'll be staying in so you can meet them?"

She looked out the window and didn't answer me. Mark was quiet as well. I drove through the snowy streets, past Mom and Dad's house and the city park that had been decorated by the local schoolchildren with various Christmas scenes and through the town square and past Norma's bare fir trees. I drove down Elmwood Lane and every house on the street had huge red bows on their mailboxes. I turned onto Boxwood and then Maple and the snow fell faster, sticking to the windshield. I drove round and round until I slowly pulled into a driveway.

"Here we are," I said. I drove up the driveway and saw Emily looking out the window. She sat up and looked through the windshield. "Do you think you could stay here?"

Girl ran to the car and barked, wanting us to get out.

"Well?" I said, "Girl's waiting for an answer. Do you think you could stay here?" I asked, watching her face. Mark grabbed her and pulled her onto the front seat.

She threw her arms around my neck.

Lynn McSwain had said he could think of several reasons why the courts wouldn't grant us guardianship. "But I can think of several more why they would," he'd said, smiling. Who knew that miracles still happen?

Five days ago I had asked God for just one day of peace in my life. I picked Emily up and kissed her face. That day had finally come.

Ten

Hope deferred makes the heart sick,
but when dreams come true,
there is life and joy.
— Proverbs 13:12

Two days later Meghan Sullivan awoke at one in the morning. "Ohh," she moaned.

Nathan jumped to his feet. "Don't move, honey," he said, pulling on a pair of jeans and a university sweatshirt he had placed nearby in case of emergency.

"Aghh," Meghan groaned, throwing her feet to the floor.

"What's wrong?" Nathan's dad asked, flipping on the light in the hallway.

"Grab the bag, Dad," Nathan said, pulling on his shoes. Jack ran for the packed overnight bag as Nathan eased Meghan through the door.

"I'm not going like this," Meghan said,

turning toward the bedroom.

"Just get in the car," Nathan said, directing her out the door again.

"I'm not going in my pajamas. I want my clothes!"

Lydia ran into Meghan's closet and pulled out a pair of maternity pants and a top. "Do these work?" she asked.

"Great," Meghan said, taking the clothes from Lydia.

Jack and Lydia scrambled back into their room to change into something for the hospital.

"Grandma's still sleeping. Should we leave her here?" Nathan asked, yelling through the closed doors.

"I'm not sleeping," his grandmother said, shuffling into the hallway. "You'd have to be deaf to sleep through all this!"

Nathan rushed Meghan into his truck and his dad, grandmother, and Lydia loaded into their car. His baby boy was finally coming!

Emily woke me that morning. Mia was being released from the hospital and she wanted to be there as she was discharged. At each visit we had seen the change in Mia; she was getting stronger every day. When Emily and Sandra and I arrived to see her leave, Dr. Andrews wasn't there. "His wife had the baby this morning," a nurse said. Emily was disappointed. I knew she wanted to see Dr. Andrews again. The nurse handed Mia to Emily and Emily made all sorts of goo-goo noises and faces.

"They told me Mia was leaving." Dr. Andrews was standing in the doorway holding a baby wrapped in a pink blanket. "I thought I'd come see her off and show everyone my new bundle."

Emily wrapped her arms around his leg, relieved to say good-bye. He leaned down so she could see the baby's face.

"She's so beautiful," I said. "What did you name her?"

"Margaret Allison. After our mothers. We'll call her Maggie." Sandra and Emily cooed at the baby.

"Welcome, Maggie," I said, bouncing her tiny hand up and down. "We hope you enjoy your stay."

"I had my heart set on a boy but I think I could get used to this," he said, kissing the baby's hand.

I looked at Dr. Andrews. His face looked so much like Mark's on the day I had Sean. "I'd ask how your Christmas was but I already know," I said, brushing Maggie's cheek. He beamed like first daddies always do and I smiled. Women go through the pain and work of labor and delivery and men parade the baby around as though they just happened to find her all snuggly and pink and beautiful.

"Mia had a very good Christmas with us," he said. "We're going to miss her around here." He put his hand on Mia's head. "She's a strong, healthy baby. We'll see her again in a few days for a checkup but I don't anticipate any problems."

"How was your Christmas, Emily?"

Emily held up the cross her mother had given her. "I got this."

"Isn't that beautiful," he said, rocking Maggie on his shoulder.

"It's from my mom."

"Well, that kind of gift is too important for Santa to deliver. An angel put that gift under the tree for you." He gave her a hug and said he hoped to see her again. Sandra and I shook his hand and thanked him for all his help and I watched as he left the room and showed Maggie off to everyone at the nurses' station. We gathered Mia's things and made our way toward the elevator, saying good-bye to the nurses who had been so good to Mia during her stay. I watched Dr. Andrews as we waited for the elevator. Funny, Mark and I had the name

Nathan on our list when we named Sean. I looked up to see three nurses bent over the baby as Dr. Andrews watched them. My mind swirled with images and conversations from the past few days. "I got here at the crack of dawn," he said on Christmas Day. I pulled out of my purse Sean's note, which was still attached to the pocket watch. I thought I heard the doorbell at six that morning. The young doctor who told me that Sean had died was named something we'd had on our list for Sean. Was that young doctor's name Nathan? Dr. Andrews laughed at the wriggling baby in his arms. *No, it couldn't be him,* I thought. *There's no way.*

The elevator doors opened and Sandra stepped inside with Mia. "Hold on, just one second," I said, running down the hall. I ran up to Dr. Andrews. He turned to look at me. "I just wanted to say . . ." I stopped. Everyone was looking at me. "I just wanted you to know that I've been to a lot of doctors and I know when I'm around a really good one. You're one of the good ones, Dr. Andrews. Thank you for everything." I ran toward the elevator and Emily waved at him as the doors closed in front of us. If I really wanted to know the name of that young doctor who told me of Sean's death I'm sure I could make a call and discover who it was. Maybe then I'd learn if it was Dr. Andrews who left the gift on my front porch. But I wouldn't do that because as Mrs. Burke told my mother, sometimes you just need to take the blessing and run.

It was a warm June day when Roy and Barbara married in our backyard. His sons had brought an arbor and decorated it with fresh roses for the ceremony. The weather was gorgeous. "Picture perfect," the photographer kept saying. For the first time in his life Roy was speechless. He looked scared to death. He mumbled his vows and everyone in attendance strained to hear him.

"Louder," Roy's son yelled.

Roy nodded his head and repeated them with gusto.

Emily sat next to Jasmine and held her hand throughout the ceremony. Roy's daughter sang "Ave Maria" and when the minister said kiss the bride, Roy dipped Barbara and planted the longest recorded kiss in the history of wedding ceremonies. The men cheered and when Roy let Barbara up for breath he pumped his fist into the air. We all released balloons and Emily and Jasmine jumped from their seats, trying to catch the ones that were caught in the trees.

After the ceremony, Mark and Dad positioned themselves at the grill and didn't move. Dad slathered the ribs with sauce and Mark monitored the blaze. Mom and I fluttered back and forth between the deck and the kitchen refilling bowls of pasta and potato salad, refreshing trays of fresh vegetables and fruit, and carrying out countless trays of appetizers. Everyone from the office was there and all of Roy's and Barbara's families. Our deck and backyard were filled. Emily wore a purple dress she had picked out at the store herself based on how much it twirled when she spun around.

My brother, Richard, and his family arrived late in the afternoon. They were going to be with us for the next four days. "I stopped at Mom and Dad's house," he said, hugging me. "I assumed they had to be here. Are we breaking up a party?"

"Not at all," I said. "We didn't expect you till later but this is better because now I can introduce you to everyone." Emily stood behind me holding on to my waist as I hugged Nancy and their three boys. I hadn't seen Richard in over a year. He was heavier but still looked good. He peeked around me to see Emily.

"Well, hello there," he said, waving. "Patti, did you know you have something on your back?" Emily giggled and held tighter.

"There's something on my back? Get it off," I said, playing along. Richard pretended to pull Emily from me, grunting for effect.

"It won't budge," he said. "I think you'll need an operation." Emily laughed and let go. "Oh, no. It's gone now."

Emily lifted her dress and rose up on her toes, embarrassed.

Richard extended his hand. "Nice to meet you, Emily. I'm Richard, Patti's brother. So that makes me your uncle."

She smiled and twirled, looking at the ground.

"We're so happy to have you as part of the family."

She rocked back and forth on top of my feet.

"And since I'm officially your uncle that means I need a kiss. Can I have a kiss?"

She shook her head.

"You won't give me a kiss?"

She laughed.

"If you won't give me a kiss then I'll have to steal one from you!" He lunged for her and she shrieked, running through the yard. Girl followed as Richard ran in circles trying to catch Emily.

I don't know when Mark and I decided to

adopt Emily. I think I knew we would the night I met her in her home and she crawled into my lap. Mark knew it when we decorated the tree. But we put the thought out of our minds and kept it at arm's length. We were too old, too broken and too wounded to start another life. That's what we thought, but I don't think our hearts ever believed it. From the moment I turned the car around at Wesley House and drove home I knew I was in for the ride of my life. Once we became Emily's legal guardians we knew there was no way we could ever let her go. She had made a place in our lives and although she didn't look like us or have our blood in her veins, we loved her as our own. She was ours. We love her as we loved Sean, as if she were born to us. We set up her bed and framed pictures of her and her mother and put them on the dresser and hung them on the wall. We didn't want her to forget her mother and we understood, as Lynn McSwain pointed out, that Emily might have special needs in the future as a result of Tracy's death, but that's okay. Mark and I had special needs, too. We were all in this together.

"Mommy!" I turned to see Emily's feet in the air. Richard was pumping her up and down. Mark and I never told her to call us

Mom and Dad; we never discussed it with her. It was easy for her to call Mark Dad because she never had one, but it took a few months before she called me Mom. I didn't make a big deal of it in front of her but afterward I went into the bathroom and cried. We were a family.

Roy's sons tied tin cans to the back of his Dodge Stratus and we all threw birdseed as Roy helped Barbara into the car. We waved and followed them down the driveway. Roy honked the horn as Barbara swatted his hands, trying to make him stop. He was taking her to, in his words, "an undisclosed location" for two weeks. We watched them turn the corner and then we headed back toward the house. There was a lot of cleaning up to do. "I'm going to get married someday," Emily said, holding my hand and Mark's.

"Oh, no you're not," Mark said.

"Yes I am, too."

"And just who are you going to marry?"

"I'm going to marry the prince."

"Well, then, that's okay," Mark said. "Because he'll have that really big castle that your mother and I can live in when we get old. But don't ever try to bring home any other guy!"

She ran after Jasmine and they sat together

on the same swing, giggling. I leaned my head on Mark's shoulder and watched her. Who would she marry? What would she be when she grew up? How many grandchildren would we have? Mark squeezed my shoulder and kissed my face. We were both thinking the same things.

We were dreaming again.

Epilogue

> . . . each day of the journey is precious,
> yours and mine — we must strive to
> make it a masterpiece. Each day, once
> gone, is gone forever.
> — John Wooden

I watch Mia in the rearview mirror. She is holding her foot and straining to see out the window. "Where we going?" In the last year Mia has grown stronger and healthier every day. Her mother, Bridget, was put in prison for four years. She's up for parole in a year and if she's released I hope she gets her life on track.

I park on the opposite side of the square and can see sparkling ornaments glistening off the three fir trees. Norma recovered from pneumonia but was never able to decorate them again. I took Emily to Norma's home one day and we had a long visit, asking if

Mark and I could take over the job she had faithfully done for over forty years. Her hip isn't as strong as she'd like it to be so she sat in a wheelchair and watched as we decorated the trees this year. "Make sure the brightest bulbs are near the bottom of the tree so children can see them," she said, pointing as we worked. "But make sure their little hands can't get tangled in the ribbon." Emily ran from one tree to the other helping Mark and me as we climbed up and down ladders and untangled one lighting mess after another. "Beautiful! Just beautiful," Norma said, clapping her hands together on our second and final day of decorating. It's my hope that our family will always be able to continue the tradition Norma began so many years ago.

Church bells ring as I open the car door.

"Where we at?" Mia asks.

"We're going to watch Emily," I say, unbuckling her car seat. Mark left two hours ago with Emily for the Christmas pageant. In November, Emily was asked to be an angel in this year's program. Mom and I got together and created her costume ourselves and after several attempts, we finally got it right. Before she and Mark left I helped straighten her wings so they came up over her shoulders and down her back, and then positioned the halo so it hovered above her head. She was an angel. Our angel.

I lift Mia out of the car seat and hold her close to me so she'll stay warm. "Mama, where's Emwee?"

I laugh and kiss her face. I love to hear her say Emily's name. Mia's adoption was final in early fall. Emily never forgot about her sick little friend in the hospital, so when Mark and I became foster parents Mia was placed in our home. When she arrived we put her in a separate room but each night Emily wanders into Mia's room and sleeps in the bed near her crib. Although they have their moments, Emily loves her little sister. I quit my job soon after Mark and I became legal guardians to Emily. I work from time to time when I'm needed but mostly I stay home and watch Emily and Mia grow.

I enter the church and look for Mark and Emily. He waves to me from up front. "Do you have the video camera?" he asks.

I hold up the bag as he takes Mia from me.

"There's my girl," he says, holding her high above his head.

I see Emily waving to us from behind the stable and I turn on the camera. I don't want to miss a thing. I wave and keep the camera to my eye, recording her jumping and waving until someone pulls her back behind the stable again. Mom and Dad, Hal and Greta, and Roy, Barbara, and Jasmine arrive and sit behind us. They are all equipped with video cameras of their own.

We join the choir as they sing "Joy to the World" and "The First Noël" and listen as a child reads the Christmas story from the Book of Luke. The scene comes to life with Mary and Joseph and a real crying baby as Jesus. Shepherds wander throughout the aisles and, behind the set, standing on a ladder so she looks as if she's hovering, is a tiny angel spreading her wings. Mark zooms in with the video camera. "Do not be afraid," Emily says. "I bring you good news of great joy that will be for all the people." I want to stand up and cheer. We had practiced that line many times together. An older angel takes the rest of the lines and Emily looks out at us, and waves. My throat tightens and I know that tears are not far behind. I made a simple choice of driving Emily to our home one year ago, and oh, how my life has changed. God didn't shout to get my attention; I never heard His voice boom from the heavens but rather He sent a child to speak to me. In the middle of my darkest days this tiny angel held my hand

and helped me to believe again. When my faith was in shreds she reminded me that God is always here, and out of that paper-thin faith came hope. And somehow that's just how faith works: no matter how frail or fractured it may be, it will always produce hope. If we allow it.

Mia bounces up and down on my lap and I smile. Out of sorrow came these tiny gifts of joy. Our girls. I lift Mia higher so she can see Emily and she squeals. Mark puts his hand on my leg and squeezes it. While our family has increased, there is still an empty seat at our table, there are pictures that stop when Sean was eighteen, and there are still dreams of a daughter-in-law and grandchildren that will never be fulfilled. It is a loss that will always weigh on my soul but I know how to breathe again. I know how to laugh and cry and seize every ounce of life from each day because, as Sean's note reminded me, I realize the value of time and how quickly it passes.

There are weeks that I can't remember how I got here or the pain that I felt; there are other times when it rushes over me in a flood. It was a long journey. On many occasions I didn't think I'd make it, or that Mark and I would survive, but we did. And today as I watch an angel dressed in white lift her wings to sing I can say that there is Hope in this world and peace in my heart.

ABOUT THE AUTHOR

Donna VanLiere is an actress and speaker and the author of the *New York Times* bestsellers *The Christmas Shoes* and *The Christmas Blessing.* She lives with her husband and their two daughters in Franklin, Tennessee. Please visit her on the Web at www.donnavanlier.com.

The employees of Thorndike Press hope you have enjoyed this Large Print book. All our Thorndike and Wheeler Large Print titles are designed for easy reading, and all our books are made to last. Other Thorndike Press Large Print books are available at your library, through selected bookstores, or directly from us.

For information about titles, please call:

(800) 223-1244

or visit our Web site at:

www.gale.com/thorndike
www.gale.com/wheeler

To share your comments, please write:

Publisher
Thorndike Press
295 Kennedy Memorial Drive
Waterville, ME 04901